THE
ONE YOU
SHOULDN'T
TRUST

SHAY HUNTER

2   BY SHAY HUNTER

APR -- 2017

ARE YOU ON OUR EMAIL LIST?

SIGN UP ON OUR WEBSITE

www.thecartelpublications.com

OR TEXT THE WORD:

CARTELBOOKS TO 22828

FOR PRIZES, CONTESTS, ETC.

CHECK OUT OTHER TITLES BY THE CARTEL PUBLICATIONS

4   BY SHAY HUNTER

WWW.THECARTELPUBLICATIONS.COM

THE ONE YOU SHOULDN'T TRUST   5

THE ONE YOU SHOULDN'T TRUST

BY SHAY HUNTER

Library of Congress Control Number: 2017932191

ISBN 10: 1945240210

ISBN 13: 978-1945240218

Cover Design: Bookslutgirl.com

www.thecartelpublications.com
First Edition
Printed in the United States of America

What's Up Fam,

Happy 2017! 2016 was one for the books man! Crazy year, but we got through it. I'm excited about what's to come. On a serious note, I know some of you may feel we got robbed in the nation, but look at it this way, everything happens for a reason. Our ancestors went through this kind of thing and it made our community stronger and made us pull together. Remember that.

Ok, enough about that, moving on to the book in hand, "The One You Shouldn't Trust" by Ms. Shay Hunter, I was pulled into this one from the very start! This book is the perfect example of what can go wrong when you elect to be sneaky instead of acting like an adult. I loved it and I know you will enjoy it too.

With that being said, keeping in line with tradition, we want to give respect to a vet or trailblazer paving the way. In this novel, we would like to recognize:

President Barack Obama

8   BY SHAY HUNTER

We all know who President Barack Obama is so there is no explanation needed. We at The Cartel Publications would like to thank President Obama and First Lady Michelle Obama for all that they did as our leaders over the last eight years. I swear if it was possible to put them back into the White House after two terms I know we would do it for as long as he wanted to run the country. I'm extremely proud to say that in my lifetime and my sons' lifetime, we saw our first Black President and prayerfully it won't be our last. God Bless you President and Mrs. Obama and thank you.

Aight, get to it. I'll catch you in the next novel.

Be Easy!

Charisse "C. Wash" Washington
Vice President
The Cartel Publications
www.thecartelpublications.com
www.facebook.com/publishercwash
Instagram: publishercwash
www.twitter.com/cartelbooks
www.facebook.com/cartelpublications

THE ONE YOU SHOULDN'T TRUST   9

CARTEL URBAN CINEMA'S 2nd WEB SERIES

IT'LL COST YOU (Twisted Tales Season One)

NOW AVAILABLE:
YOUTUBE / STREAMING / DVD

www.youtube.com/user/tstyles74

www.cartelurbancinema.com

www.thecartelpublications.com

THE ONE YOU SHOULDN'T TRUST   11

CARTEL URBAN CINEMA'S 1st WEB SERIES

THE WORST OF US (Season One & Season Two)

NOW AVAILABLE:

YOUTUBE / STREAMING/ DVD

www.youtube.com/user/tstyles74

www.cartelurbancinema.com

www.thecartelpublications.com

BY SHAY HUNTER

CARTEL URBAN CINEMA'S 1st MOVIE

PITBULLS IN A SKIRT - THE MOVIE

www.cartelurbancinema.com and
www.amazon.com
www.thecartelpublications.com

THE ONE YOU SHOULDN'T TRUST   13

#TheOneYouShoudn'tTrust

BY SHAY HUNTER

Not everybody was there that cool night in October when nine people died. But that didn't stop them from reporting the news like they were there, in the room, watching us.

I hate that type shit.

Yes people lost their lives and yes the night started out as a celebration. Still, there was a reason for everything and only those who lived in our apartment knew the details.

But since you're interested let me sum up what people looking from the outside in believe...

Take four sexy roommates, all of us different in every way. Now imagine one of us is short, light skin and with an ass so phat it's hard for men and women not to look twice. I'm talking about a body that makes insecure bitches jealous.

Can you see it?

Well that's me and my name is Tabitha 'Macbeth' Holmes. But my roommates call me, 'The One You Shouldn't Trust'.

I don't see things that way. But after hearing my story you can tell me what you think ...

CHAPTER ONE

TABITHA

Okay I admit, I can be a little extra but it's in my blood. For instance right now I'm prepping for the one-year anniversary party my roommates and me are throwing in a few days. We're celebrating the day we met and rented this luxury four-bedroom apartment together.

Ain't that cute!

Anyway, this kitchen is crowded, most of the stuff I have to cook in advance and put in the fridge. So here I am, standing in front of the stove working on all the edible baked goods. That's the respectable term for the weed treats I made. We have weed brownies, cookies and candy. And since I had a little THC oil left in the pan I was thinking about making weed omelets and bacon for breakfast.

People who don't know me think I overdo it in the kitchen but me and my roommates were once gonna start a business call *Me and my Bud's* when DC, first announced that weed was legal. That's the reason the large green and white sign is lying against the wall in the living room with the name of our business. It's a reminder of dreams never fulfilled.

Which is perfectly okay with me.

Anyway, right before we attempted to get a small store, we were denied due to all of the restrictions DC placed on us. We soon found out that the only drug dealer in DC was the government and so we had to get rid of our entrepreneur plans.

It never stopped me from cooking because for some reason it relaxed me and helped me keep out of trouble.

I removed the brownies from the oven and wiped my hands on my tight blue jeans before taking a big breath. I was almost done for the day and was about to cook breakfast when there was a knock. I glanced down at myself really quickly to make sure I didn't look a mess and opened the door. When I saw who was outside I looked behind me and back at him.

It was Dandre, my roommate Barby's boyfriend. "Hurry up in here." I grabbed his hand, glanced behind me again before yanking him inside.

He hugged me and rushed into the apartment. About 5'11, I always joked at how much he looked like the rapper 6Lack with a low haircut. His chocolate black skin was covered with neat baby dreads surrounding his face. He wasn't my type but he certainly wasn't the ugliest boy in the room either.

"Damn, girl," he looked me up and down. "Why you moving so fast?" He rubbed his hands together as if he had all the time in the world.

I grabbed his hand again and took him into the kitchen and when I was sure my roommates were not coming I said, "So let me look at it." I was so excited I couldn't stand still. "And hurry up before she come out here and sees it for herself."

Slowly he removed a red box from his designer blue jeans and popped open the top. A beautiful gold ring with a nice enough diamond was nestled inside. "So what you think about this knot? It's decent or nah?"

I removed it from him, took out the ring and slipped it on my finger. It fit perfectly. "Oh my, gawd, Dandre! You went all out!" I covered my mouth as I eyed the beauty. "It's perfect."

"Stop fucking around."

"I'm serious!" I took the ring off and stuffed it back into the plush box. "I mean it's really nice, Dandre."

"Would you wear something like this? Be honest!"

My eyes widened. "For sure I would!"

"So you don't think it's too small do you?" He stuffed the box into his pocket. "Because the last thing I need is her getting cold feet and not accepting my proposal." He shrugged. "For real, this the first time I'm thinking about being on some married shit with a broad. I need to make sure everything is legit, Tabitha."

"You gotta think more positive than that." I crossed my arms over my chest. "If you don't believe she'll say yes she probably won't." I paused. "But trust me, after seeing this she *will* say yes."

He looked at me. "How you know?"

"Because we have the same tastes and she loves me to death." I wiped my long black hair from my face. "So let's just say I know her like the back of my hand. Is that good enough for you?"

He smiled and hugged me again.

CHAPTER TWO
BARBY

After seeing Tabitha all up in my nigga's grill I closed the door and faced my roommates Kaden and Paris who were in my room. "I can't stand that bitch! I'm telling yah some real shit!"

"What you talking about now?" Paris asked as if I was a fly, getting on her nerves again.

Paris was sitting on the edge of my bed and Kaden was on the floor between her legs getting her hair braided for the party this weekend. Our place had plenty space but they were always in mine.

We had four rooms with two bedrooms in the front and two in the back of the apartment but I had more luxuries so everyone loved spending more time here. I had a 62-inch TV on the wall, a Bose sound system hooked up to it and a refrigerator stocked with beer, wine and snacks. Well most of the time anyway.

I guess if I were them I would prefer to be in here too.

When I moved closer to them I wiped my long red faux locs out of my face and stuffed my hands into my thin grey sweatpants, which I was wearing without panties to be comfortable around the apartment. "She doing it again, yah. Pushing up."

Kaden looked at me before Paris pushed her head back down so she could finish braiding her natural long hair. "What yo red ass talking 'bout now?"

"And where's my juice?" Paris asked, sectioning a new part for a braid in Kaden's scalp. "I thought you were goin' to the big fridge since yours is dry." She giggled to herself.

"That's what I'm trying to say. I opened the door to get it and I saw Tabitha huddled up with Dandre in the kitchen. Whispering and shit." I threw my hands up. "Like...what the fuck is that about? Why she in my nigga's face so much lately?"

Paris stopped braiding and they both looked at me. "Why didn't you ask her instead of complaining to us?"

"Why? So he could be mad at me?" I pointed to myself.

Paris shook her head and started braiding again. "Wait...I'm playing but you know she would never do nothing like that to you. Right?"

My eyes widened. "Do I?"

Paris shook her head, her long curls softly brushing against the sides of her face. "You need to relax cuz don't nobody want Dandre's ugly ass but you."

Kaden giggled and held her stomach. "I don't mean to be laughing but she right. Stop with all the conspiracies, Barby. Tabitha real people and she never did anything to make us feel different."

I grabbed the chair I had against the wall and moved it closer before flopping down in front of them so I can see their eyes. I swear they had me heated. "So yah gonna act like her record perfectly clean?" I asked. "Really?"

"Like I said she never did nothing to me," Paris shrugged.

"Well let me remind you." I paused. "Do you remember the time we had the pool party down the rec center last year? For Kaden's birthday?" I paused and waited for their answer. "Oh don't act like yah forgot?"

Kaden rolled her eyes and scratched her chocolate nose. "Oh yeah, but I thought we said we would never talk about that again?" She giggled. "So why you keep bringing it up?"

"I'm serious!" I frowned. "She was the one who suggested skinny dipping even though all our niggas were there and we said no. But what did she do? Jump her freshly made fake ass into the pool *naked*...causing each of our niggas to break they necks watching. She pressed for attention!"

"The girl got a bad body," Kaden shrugged. "I'd be running around butt naked too."

Paris giggled.

"Not everybody like men and women like your dyke ass, Kaden," I said. "I was highly offended when she did that in front of Dandre."

"Okay you got the one scenario," Paris nodded. "But give me another one."

"I got two more." I pointed at them. "Remember that time she suggested we play Truth or Dare? And she positioned the questions so she got to kiss each one of our niggas in the mouths." I threw my hands up in the air. "I mean come on, yah, it's right in front of your eyes. Why I got to spell it out?"

Paris exhaled. "Okay, another one," Paris said.

"What?" I frowned.

"You said you had another one so tell us some more."

I sat back in my chair and it squeaked. "Wait...are yah believing me or not?" I paused. "Cuz I'm not gonna be talking to myself 'round here."

"Bitch, just finish telling the story!" Kaden yelled.

I sighed. "There's plenty other situations but I'll tell you this one. Remember that time she begged Lakota to take her shopping for Christmas because her nigga was gone all day?"

Kaden frowned because he was her boyfriend and suddenly things weren't funny anymore. I could see her eyes brighten a little and she scratched her face again. "Yeah...they left at 1:00pm and didn't come back 'til 10:00 that night," Kaden said.

"Yeah...I'm not gonna lie, that got my eyebrows rising too but it was Christmas Eve," Paris said. "Everybody knows the stores were packed. Maybe you making a big deal out of nothing."

These bitches were being stupid on purpose. A bitter taste filled my mouth. "So running around butt naked around yah's niggas and kissing them in the mouths is nothing? That's basically what yah telling me." I looked at both of them.

Paris waved the air. "All I know is she's never done anything to me and I'm not about to change my mind because you letting your nigga stay in the kitchen and hold court with her."

I glared at her. "I swear yah bitches green. Both of you." I pointed at them.

"You love drama, Barby," Paris said. "You like the rest of them red bitches in the world, who think somebody 'spose to give you something just cause you cute." She waved her hand. "Yah all the same."

She sound dumb as shit! "You red too, hoe! It be different if Kaden said it but you got a nerve."

"I'm a little browner, due to my father fucking my mother from behind so much...so it's different." She shrugged. "At least that's what they told me."

I frowned. "What the fuck?"

"All I'm saying is that you love conspiracies and you know how I can prove it?" Paris continued.

"No I don't."

"Your nigga is out in the living room right now and instead of getting him from the *She Devil* you in here telling us about, you talking our heads off." She paused. "If you really thought she was dangerous you would be out there snatching her hair from her scalp. By the roots!"

KNOCK. KNOCK.

I got up and walked toward the door. They weren't talking about anything anyway.

When I opened the door I was staring at my boyfriend's face. My lip twitched but I tried to hide it. "Hey, sexy." Dandre pulled me toward him with his big hands, wrapped his arms around my waist and kissed me on the lips. It was a wet minty one. The kind you smelled for about thirty minutes.

"What you in here doing?" He looked behind me. "You ain't hear me come in and call your name?" He snaked his fingers between the crack of my ass and grabbed a handful.

"Nah, I been trying to get these bitches out my room but they won't leave," I kissed him again and inhaled his cologne.

"Well you gonna be getting me out this pussy in a minute," he said seductively. "With your sexy ass."

I couldn't help but grin. "I'd never want to—"

"Ewww, get the fuck out already!" Paris said jokingly. "Yah, doing the most. We ain't taking no pictures for the Gram."

Dandre laughed and walked out leaving me alone with them for a few seconds more. "Remember what I said." I whispered. "Keep your eyes open because I don't trust that bitch. Not around my nigga and yah shouldn't either. I'm just saying."

I closed the door and walked out.

CHAPTER THREE
KADEN

When Barby left the room I stood up and sat in the chair she was sitting in to think about what she was really trying to tell us about Tabitha. Stuff did seem weird with her lately. At first I didn't think much of Barby's claims but now I wasn't so sure about it.

"What you doing, girl?" Paris picked up her phone and scrolled the screen with her thumb. "I'm not done your hair! You better come on before you be getting it braided by one of Barby's cousins again. And you know you hate that shit." She tossed her cell on the bed and stared at me. "Well are you gonna sit back down or not?"

I pointed at her. "So what you think 'bout what she just said? About Tabitha playing herself like a whore in front of our niggas?"

"I'm not gonna be on your head all night, Kaden." She picked up her cell phone again, sent a text and sat it back on the bed. "So you better sit back down while I'm in the mood."

"No for real, listen!" I scooted closer. "I'm really starting to play the tapes back in my head. Tabitha really is a mess and Barby made a lot of good points. I think we tried to push a lot of stuff she does to the side because the apartment is real nice and we like being here but I'm not about to let her take my nigga. Not for no fireplace in the living room."

Paris stood up and walked away from me. "Why we gotta ruin what we have here? This the first time I had roommates I liked and there ain't been no drama. And now just because Barby don't trust her dude we shouldn't trust ours? Don't forget Barby's the same one who conveniently forgets to put her robe on at night when she runs to the bathroom. I mean how many times Lakota seen Barby's butt cheeks? You told me he saw them the other night." She paused. "Does that make it any different?"

"No it just—"

"Please don't let that girl fuck up your living situation, Kaden." She paused. "I know for a fact you ain't been in a good mood. I mean I don't know what's happening but I bet it's because stuff ain't been going good in your world with your man. Don't add extra by—"

When a rock came crashing through Barby's window we both jumped. I rushed to it and looked outside. Little Chris was laughing hysterically holding his stomach. He's got to be the worst kid in the world.

He was about to try and get away on his bicycle when my boyfriend Lakota got out of his grey BMW and grabbed him off his feet. The kid looked like he wanted to shit on himself and I was so glad because he had it coming. He threw rocks a lot. That's the one thing I hate about living on the second floor, stupid things like that happened all the time.

"What's wrong with that little nigga?" Paris asked standing beside me. "He ain't got nothing better to do than to throw rocks at windows? I should fuck him up." She paused. "And what Lakota doing outside in the car?" She looked at me. "Why he ain't come upstairs?"

I frowned. "I'm gonna find out." I walked toward the door.

"Well you better hurry up back to get your hair done!"

BY SHAY HUNTER

The air was a little cool when I approached my boyfriend but the moment he saw me walking toward him he looked irritated. Like I had done something wrong. "What you doing out here, bae?" I smiled and tried to kiss him but he turned his head like my breath stunk. "Damn, it's like that?"

"I came with Dandre." He pulled out his phone and started texting like I was a non-factor. "I think he still upstairs with Barby. We got some stuff to rap about so I'm not staying long."

I wiped his neat dreads off his shoulders and looked up at him. He's covered in tats but my favorite is the one on his neck with my name. "Lakota, why you acting different with me? It seems like whenever I wanna get in touch with you, you ain't got no time but you do for Dandre."

He turned his head away. "Ain't nothing wrong." His stare remained on his cell phone. "Stop tripping."

"Lakota...please. Is it about your mother passing away or—"

"If that's what you want it to be about it's whatever," he said cutting me off.

I slammed my hand over his screen to stop him from looking at it and to look at me instead. "Can you please look at me?"

He sighed. "Why everything gotta be about something, Kaden? Why can't you let some shit go?"

"Because I know you and — "

"I got a new girl, aight?!"

I stepped back. "A new girl? Fuck does that mean?"

He sat on the hood of his car. "Come on, bae, don't act like you haven't been feeling the breakdown. I barely come over here and when I do I'm with Dandre on business."

I positioned myself between his legs. "The breakdown? Is that before or after you tasted my pussy?" He shoved me backwards and I rushed him and slapped his face.

Angry, Lakota grabbed my wrist and squeezed it tightly. My fingers ran cold. "I could've killed you just now but I'm not gonna do that."

"You gonna do something, Lakota! You not about to play with me like this!" Tears filled the wells of my eyes. "I been fucking you, loving you and giving you all my time for months." I pointed at the ground. "And if I gotta, I'm willing to fight for you."

"It's over. Ain't no need in keep talking about a situation that's dead."

"Well I'm not letting you go, Lakota. You got my name tattooed on your body and I got yours on mine!" I raised my sleeve so he could see LAKOTA going down my arm. "Tats don't come off! We forever. Remember that."

He shook his head. "I'm just gonna be honest, you not my type."

My eyebrows lowered and pinched together. "Not your type? But we been together all this time. When this happen?"

"Look at how you dress?" he raised his voice. "Like a dude. You know how embarrassing it is to walk down the street with you? Only for people to think I'm gay cause you dressed like a nigga? Especially when your hair is braided like that." He waved his hand. "But it ain't like I ain't tell you before so don't fake dumb."

My eyebrows rise. "A dude!" My heart thumped loudly and I wondered if he could hear it. "A…a dude, Lakota? That's how you think I look? I thought you liked when we played basketball together. Love and Basketball remember? That's our favorite movie."

He looked up and down the block, I guess to see if people were watching us. He cared too much about what people thought and that turned me off sometimes. "Fuck I tell you about show boating in public? That's another reason I don't deal with you."

"Showboating?" My fists clenched and I was playing in my mind how it would feel to box him. As mad as I was if I tried hard I think I could take him. "Nigga, I sucked your dick almost every day since I been with you. And I'm showboating? You serious?"

"Look, if it ain't working it ain't working and there's nothing you can do to get me to change my mind." He folded his arms across his chest and looked away from me.

I felt like I had been gut punched especially since I loved him so much I thought about him everyday. Yeah I played with girls when I was in high school but I hadn't touched one since I graduated five years ago.

Yeah I'm tomboyish and prefer my hair in braids instead of weaves. Yes, I'm a sneaker head who wears large sweatpants and sports bras without makeup. But if I'm gay that must make Teyana Taylor gay too because people say we look just alike.

"Now get outta my face before I really hurt your feelings." He took his phone from his pocket and started texting someone again.

I could feel my blood boiling.

You know what, he got me all the way fucked up. Whenever he's deep in this pussy he says he can't see me with anyone else but now he don't care anymore? I took off one of my Jordan One's and then the other.

"What you doing?" He asked.

"Since you think I'm a nigga let me see how much attention I'll get when my ass is out." I shrugged. "I'm one of the dudes right? So who will care?"

"Don't be stupid, Kaden!" He said through clenched teeth.

He moved away from me and looked up the block again. "Nah, if you say I'm such a boy then if I'm naked it shouldn't be a problem? Niggas should walk right by me and not look."

"Fuck! You always on some stupid shit instead of letting things go." He pointed at me.

I removed my shirt and then my black sweatpants. "Nah, if I'm a dude then—"

Suddenly he smacked me so hard I forgot what I was doing. Then he grabbed my shoulders, shook me once and then squeezed tightly. "Put your clothes on before I beat yo ass out here. LIKE...YOU...A...NIGGA!"

"La—"

He gripped me harder and through clenched teeth said, "You think I'm fucking around? Put your clothes on before I crash your chest." He picked up my sneaker, my shirt and my pants and stuffed them into my hands.

When I looked up Paris was in the window watching it all.

CHAPTER FOUR

PARIS

I slammed the window and shook my head. Afterwards I swept up the small glass from the broken window and called the maintenance man to come fix it, which meant he was gonna charge us I'm sure.

Wow!

Kaden is off the chain out there.

I'm so sick of them fighting and getting back together that when she tells me they're broken up I don't even listen anymore. They'll be back together before —

My phone rung and I snatched it off the bed, lied down and answered it. Staring at the ceiling I said, "Hey, sexy. I was waiting on you to hit my phone when I texted earlier."

Maceo chuckled. "I thought I was 'spose to call you that."

"What? Sexy?" I giggled. "You can still say it if you want."

"Hey, sexy."

I wiggled my foot and tried to hide my smile but he has me going crazy over him. This nigga does everything to me, mentally and physically. "I miss you, Maceo! When you coming over? I feel like it's been months."

"And I figured yah be getting ready for that party. What you want with me? I'll just be in the way."

My eyes widened. "You mean besides some dick?" I paused. "Boy, don't play with me. I would prefer you over any party. Anyway, I thought you were coming. Don't ruin my day."

"You wild..." He chuckled. "But I'm just fucking around."

"You better be. So when you get back in town?"

"I'm actually at the airport now. I should land in Baltimore in about a hour and a half. Maybe a little longer."

"So you have people sitting around you?" I asked seductively. "Or are you all alone? Like me?"

He chuckled. "Yeah I'm solo. Why? What you gonna do about it?"

"Put me on Video Time." I begged. "So I can see your face."

"You gonna let me see them titties too?"

I giggled. "Of course I'm gonna let you see these titties." He hung up and when my phone rang again I was looking at his face. Maceo is so fine. Out of all of our boyfriends mine is the better looking if you ask me. Well, Chaviv, Tabitha's dude is pretty cute too.

Anyway, Maceo's hair is long and curly like mine and he wears it in a man bun on top of his head, which I love. There's nothing about him that's not perfect. The way he dresses. The way he smells and most of all the way he fucks me.

I sat up. "You ready?"

"Yeah, sexy," he licked his lips. "Show me them things."

With the camera on my chest, I unbuttoned my pink and red polo shirt and exposed my red lace bra. Then I pulled out my left breast and ran my pink tongue over the nipple really slowly. It tingled and judging by how he bit his lip I could tell he loved the show.

"Damn...do...that...shit,' He said slowly. "Don't forget the other one too, beautiful."

"I ain't forget," I winked.

Next I dipped into the bra and pulled out my other breast, running my tongue over it too. Suddenly my body heated up and I was horny as usual when we played this game. Maceo was a construction worker, which took him around the world on different jobs sometimes. Because of it I didn't get a chance to see him as much as I wanted but when we did it was like fire between us.

We had a lot of secrets.

There was another side to Maceo that only I knew about. A freakier side, which brought us together in the first place. I went about finding him differently. When I was looking for a man I searched this website based on a fetish I have. One that I'm ashamed of.

The moment we met and did our thing we'd been together ever since. Maceo was the only man I could see myself marrying but my heart told me something would happen. I felt like we wouldn't last and it made me sick sometimes.

The last time I was in love with a man he ended up leaving me for a chick he got pregnant back in high school. I was devastated for a week. I started dating again and the dude after him I was feeling just stop calling me after six months.

Basically I had a bad run with men.

Something told me this time would be different but my heart said I couldn't be sure.

"Take the camera lower, Paris... Let me see that kitten too." Maceo said. "Open it up." He bit his lip.

Looking at the bedroom door, since I was still in Barby's room, I hoped she didn't come inside and ruin our game. I heard voices outside and smelled weed edibles so I figured she was cooking and they were tasting the goods. I guess playing with my pussy for a second wouldn't hurt much.

Stuffing my pink fingernail into my waiting body I positioned the camera so he could see it clearly. Then I fingered myself until I was so juicy it was dripping on Barby's sheets. When I snuck a peek at the screen I could tell he was in a bathroom stall and figured he was beating his dick.

My baby was as kinky as me.

I smiled to myself and continued to work my pussy until I was so slick it looked like I pissed on Barby's bed. "Yeah, just like that....just like that...," he directed. "I'm 'bout to cum."

In and out in and out I fingered myself and slid my index finger over my clit to the point where it was too tingly to be touched and within seconds I came. When

I looked at the phone he was breathing heavily staring at the screen. "I'm gonna fuck you up, girl." He said out of breath. "Why you do that to me?"

I giggled and pulled my clothes together before someone came in. "You asked for it and I complied." I winked.

"Well you came through. I know that shit." He tossed the paper in the toilet and walked out the stall. At the sink he washed one hand and then the other so he could maintain control of the phone. "That pussy just as pretty as ever." He paused. "Damn, I can't wait to feel you."

"So since you like what you saw, does that mean I get to see you tonight?" I paused. "Cuz I don't think I can wait until the weekend, Maceo."

"After all that you know I'm coming over." He scratched his scalp. "The moment this plane lands I'll be looking for part two."

I giggled and then remembered what Barby said about Tabitha being sneaky. Her suspicious words didn't get me like it did Kaden and Barby but still, I decided to check with him. "Let me ask you something and I want you to give me an honest opinion."

"Shoot." I could see he was back in the terminal and waiting on his flight.

"Did Tabitha ever come on to you? Like, try to fuck you behind my back or something?"

"What?" His eyes widened and he seemed disgusted with the question. "How you sound?"

"I'm serious!"

"Didn't you tell me she was the best roommate you ever had? And that you liked living over there?"

"I did, but what does that have to do with my question?" I sighed. "Something came up today and I want to know if she's ratchet like I'm hearing." I shrugged. "Plus it shouldn't matter what I said to you in the past, Maceo. I'm asking you now."

He shook his head and was doing his best to make me feel dumb. "I don't know what's going on but females love to keep up shit. That much I know."

"What that 'spose to mean?"

"Don't let nobody change your opinion about somebody when it's already been made, Paris. That's gump shit, bae."

"It's not that—"

"I've never heard you say a negative word about her to me. Then all of a sudden she's an enemy? Relax, man."

My stomach rumbled a little upon hearing how hard he was coming at me. "Wow, you coming at me hard. Sure you not crushing on her all of a sudden?"

Suddenly my phone went to a screensaver. It was a picture of me and Maceo on the beach last summer. I figured he hung up on me so I called back and the moment he answered I said, "I'm sorry, Maceo, please don't hang up! I don't want the fighting shit between me and you! Please forgive me!"

"Yeah, whatever."

I heard a door close in the living room but I maintained my focus on the phone. "Do you forgive me?"

He looked away like he was thinking about hanging up on me again. "Look, we just had a nice time, Paris. I care about you. But don't put me in the middle of your female games. And don't fuck up your situation in that apartment because of some busy bodied chick."

"You right." I exhaled. "So I guess you not coming over tonight now huh?"

"I told you I would so I am." All of a sudden I heard a loud noise in the living room. It sounded like something crashed against the wall and screaming followed. "What the fuck was all that?" He asked in a concerned tone. "Everything okay?"

"I don't know but I'm gonna find out."

"Hit me back the moment you can. Let me know you're safe, Paris. And don't get involved in nothing that's not your business." He pointed at me. "It's probably Barby kicking up shit."

"Okay, Maceo."

I ended the call and ran to the door, flinging it open. My eyes widened when I saw all of the blood in the living room.

My roommates were standing around looking crazy.

What happened?

CHAPTER FIVE

TABITHA

MOMENTS EARLIER

After placing my last batch of weed caramel candy in the refrigerator, I turned the radio up a little when I heard 'The Drop' by Bro Safari come on the speakers. When I was done I wrapped my hair in a loose bun on top of my head and twerked a little because it was my favorite trap song.

"Girl, cut all that shit out," Barby said.

I giggled. "Don't be jealous." I danced harder, my ass popping up and down. "Plus you know that's one of my favorite songs."

She rolled her eyes playfully and I walked over to her on the sofa where she was seated next to Dandre. I flopped on his right and she got up and squeezed between us, her long red locs slapping me in the face in the process.

She bony as fuck so her but bone stabbed me in the thigh and I rubbed it to stop the pain. "Damn, girl!" I frowned. "Why you being so extra?" That was doing a

BY SHAY HUNTER

lot but that's Barby's way so I wasn't surprised in the least.

"Ain't no need in you sitting so close to my nigga," She said as she nudged me with her hand on my thigh, a smile on her face but hate in her eyes. "You got plenty room on the couch. Over there." She pointed far away from them and I scooted over a little.

Dandre laughed and shook his head. "Why you being jealous? You know Tab cool as fuck."

"I know she cool," she kissed him sloppily, like she was putting on shows for me. "I was just fucking with her that's all." She looked at me and said, "Where Chaviv? He should've been here by now. I thought we were gonna play some cards or something."

"You know how he be, girl," I shrugged. "I called earlier and he said the same thing he always does. He'll get at me when he gets here. I don't worry 'bout rushing him no more." I laughed thinking about how he loved to fake hard, knowing all the while if I dumped his ass he would be lost. "But the moment I leave him and go out without him there's a problem. I did that the other day and—"

BANG! BANG! BANG!

"Fuck!" Dandre said leaping from the sofa before moving toward the door. "I'm in here messing with yah and I forgot I left the nigga Lakota outside. Bet he think I did the shit on purpose too. Watch. Last thing I feel like is dealing with this petty nigga. He liable to fuck up my high right about now."

He opened the door and Lakota stomped inside with Kaden behind him looking like she wasn't loved. I could tell they'd been fighting without even talking to her and was sure she'd give me the run down later.

I stood up and walked toward them.

"Why you leave me outside, nigga?" Lakota yelled at Dandre, his fists balled up in knots. "You could've said you was gonna be in here a little longer."

"First off you the one who wanted to come out here with me. Remember? I told you we could talk about that situation later." He paused. "Now relax, I lost track of time and —"

"Nigga, you ain't lose track of time." Lakota looked around at the beer cans on the table. "Seems to me you in here chillin'." He stared around and even glanced at our business sign leaning on the wall. "Now are we gonna talk 'bout this now or not? I'm not fucking around nigga. I came over here as a man to get at you one on one. I could've handled it another way."

Dandre frowned and wiped his hand down his face like he had enough already. "First off you act like your girl don't live here," Dandre shrugged. "You could've came in anytime so stop tripping."

"NIGGA, I CAME HERE TO TALK BUSINESS!" Lakota yelled louder. "With you! Why I gotta keep saying it?" he pointed at him. "If you ask me it seems like you dodging and I got a problem with that. Maybe I should let the streets handle it?"

Dandre's nostrils flared. "My nigga, you threatening me? Cuz that's what it sounds like."

Lakota stood stronger and stared him down. For a second neither one of them said a word. They never went at each other like this and most of the time you couldn't find one without the other. Far as I knew they ran a trap together.

"If I was threatening you I wouldn't be here." He paused. "But you would've felt my heat. Now I'm asking again, what you wanna do? Talk now or later?"

"Dandre, what's going on?" Barby said, her body trembling. "Yah cool right? This ain't nothing serious."

THE ONE YOU SHOULDN'T TRUST   49

"You know what, let's rap outside." Dandre said. "You grabbing an audience now and it don't even call for all this."

"Fuck it, now I want to talk about it here." Lakota responded, folding his arms over his chest. The vein in his temple pulsating. "I ain't got time for the other shit."

"Bae, why you acting all crazy?" Kaden asked placing her hand on his forearm. "At first I thought I was the only problem but you tripping on everybody." She giggled, I guess to break the mood but no one smiled.

Not even me.

This was serious.

"Kaden, I'm not talking to you," he warned, pointing a stiff finger in her face. "I could give a fuck about all that you were rapping about outside. I done said all I'm going to about that. Now sit the fuck down before I—"

"Hold up, why you talking to that female like that?" Dandre stepped up closer to Lakota. "Now I said we could rap outside."

Lakota laughed. "You mean to tell me I been outside all day and now you wanna be in here acting like Mr. Save A Ho for my bitch? Tend to yo freak over there." He pointed at her.

I think he went too far.

Dandre stole him in the lips and the next thing I know they were rolling around on my living room floor trying to kill each other. After Dandre's blow, Lakota answered it by stealing him in the lower jaw, forcing him against the TV. All I could do was hope they didn't mess up anything.

For now everything was still in tact.

Me, Kaden and Barby tried to break them up as best we could but things were way out of control now. Luckily nothing had broken yet but I was sure if I didn't manage to stop them it would be happening soon.

"Come on, yah!" I yelled. "You gonna get us put out! My neighbors might call the police or something."

They didn't stop.

And the next thing I knew Lakota pulled out a knife and aimed at Dandre. I didn't know he had it on him. Kaden screamed and Barby was in hysterics on the sofa, like she was praying to God to break this situation up.

"Lakota, what the fuck is wrong with you?" Kaden yelled with her palms in his direction. "Why you wilding out? Put that shit up. This your boy."

"She's right, Lakota," Barby sobbed. "It's one thing to be in a disagreement and a whole nother to be stabbing somebody. What could be that bad yah going at each other like this?"

"He know what could be this bad," Lakota continued, his eyes glaring in Dandre's direction. "That's why he should've stepped outside instead of hanging in here like I asked. None of this would've happened. Now shit out of hand."

"I'm listening now, man," Dandre said calmly with raised hands, palms in Lakota's direction. "But you don't want to hurt the girls do you? So be easy and put that shit up. Aight, man?" He slowly moved toward Lakota. "Who carries a knife anyway?"

"Don't play me, nigga," Lakota continued as my roommates and I stood around and watched everything go down. "You done took me somewhere I didn't want to go. Now I —,"

Dandre must be high off my edibles because he charged at him despite Lakota having the weapon in his hand. He misjudged though because Lakota saw him coming and poked at his hand, tearing into the flesh of his finger.

When I heard someone scream I turned around and saw Paris coming out Barby's room. I wanted her to stop yelling but she got louder. Blood was all over my floor, the TV screen and even the bottle of Kaden's sweatpants.

"What's going on?" Paris yelled covering her mouth. "What yah out here doing?"

"YOU CUT ME, NIGGA!" Dandre screamed holding his hand. "YOU FUCKING CUT ME!"

It looked like Lakota had come back to his senses because he dropped the knife and walked up to him. "I'm sorry, man," Lakota said, his jaw hung as he eyed all the blood. "I didn't mean to do it but...shit got out of control."

I ran to the kitchen to get a white towel and wrapped it around his hand. "Let me get you to the hospital." I grabbed my purse sitting on the table and my car keys.

"I'll take him myself, Tabitha but thank you anyway," Barby said.

My eyebrows rose. "But you don't have a car."

"Well I'm going with you! But I should definitely be with *my man*."

"Whatever you wanna do," I said rolling my eyes as me, Barby, Lakota, Dandre and Kaden rushed out, with Paris staying behind.

CHAPTER SIX

PARIS

I was still trembling.

I gotta change my panties because I think I peed on myself I was so scared. When I rushed to the bathroom and removed them I noticed I did but they were also damp because my pussy was wet from messing with Maceo.

I washed myself up, slipped on clean underwear and stared in the mirror in the bathroom at my reflection. I can't believe all that just went down. What is happening in this place?

I tried to hit Maceo to tell him I was okay but he didn't answer his phone. And I'm glad because for real I didn't feel like talking at the moment. Maybe he was in the air and I needed him to hurry to me.

Barby texted me and said that Lakota stabbed Dandre but that things were okay between them. When I asked her what they were fighting for she said neither wanted to tell anybody. But they have been friends for so long that it messed up my mind. It doesn't make any sense.

Still, I decided to leave it alone.

I got other shit on my mind and getting in Lakota and Dandre's biz is not one of them. I'm sure it was drug related anyway.

With my nerves a little calmer I grabbed the mop, Pine Sol and filled a bucket with hot water to clean up the blood. Believe it or not I'm used to cleaning up bodily fluids because I worked in a hospital for a little while before I got a job with Barby and Kaden at the electric company in customer service.

When the blood was gone I straightened the living room. I couldn't stand trash so I picked up the beer cans off the table, the trash on the floor and then vacuumed. I will say when it comes to cleanliness I do it best but I don't mind.

It helped calm my nerves.

When my cell phone rang I answered it with a smile when I saw it was Maceo. "Hey, baby. I fucking miss you so much. You wouldn't believe all the shit that happened over here tonight. Lakota —"

"Open the door."

My heart dropped.

He was here!

I dropped the vacuum handle and my phone, pulled the front door open and jumped on him. Landing kisses all over his face, cheek and neck my heart was beating a mile a minute. "You're here! I thought you wouldn't be back until 6:00 in the evening! Oh, Maceo! Thanks for coming straight over like you said."

He chuckled, slapped my ass and closed the door, all with me straddling him. "You wild as shit." He looked into my eyes. I loved when he did that because it meant he saw me. "You know that right?"

"Maceo, I'm serious." I exhaled. "I missed you. And if I told you what happened earlier you wouldn't believe me."

He put me down. "As long as you don't tell me you had a fight with your roommate again I'm good."

I eased off of him and crossed my arms over my chest. "No I didn't fight her, Maceo."

I understand he doesn't want my living situation messed up. But sometimes I feel like he cares about her more than he should. Now that I think about it, everybody's dude seemed to care what Tabitha thought about stuff. In my mind even if I had a beef with her he should be by my side.

"Was the fight about Tabitha, Paris? Because I know you had some issues with her earlier."

"No, it wasn't about Tabitha. It was Dandre and Lakota." I sighed. "From what I was told Lakota stabbed him."

"What the fuck?" His eyes widened. "So Lakota found out huh?" He shook his head and my heart thumped. What did he know about this? My dude wasn't in the street like my roommates' dudes so I was confused.

"Found out what?"

Maceo wheeled his suitcase into my room, walked back out and flopped on the sofa. I could tell he was exhausted and probably hungry. "I don't know a lot, Paris. All I'm gonna say is word around the city is that Dandre got into a shoot out with some niggas and hit Lakota's cousin. He's dead. Died last night in the hospital."

My eyes widened and I sat next to him. My mind started working overtime. Would Kaden and Barby stop talking to each other too? "What? You serious, Maceo? Because they were best friends as far as I knew. How could this happen?"

He scratched his head and his long hair came down his shoulders. It was so much thicker and prettier than mine and Tabitha's. "Wouldn't play like that, baby girl. I was fucked up when I heard it too." He shrugged. "But the streets takes friendships like the devil takes souls. You know that already." He rubbed my thigh.

I ran my hand down my face. "No wonder he stabbed him."

Maceo shrugged. "If you wanna be honest Lakota's people had it coming. They stay kicking up shit on other niggas blocks so Dandre and his cousins had enough. Old boy robbed niggas. Fucked other niggas broads. Bamma's be claiming they don't care and it's bros before hoes but the dead bodies falling in DC say tell another story."

"You don't believe that," I said. "That he had it coming."

"I'm not saying he deserved to be killed but I understand how it happened, Paris. That's all I'm trying to get through to you. It's all street shit and it never stops." He grabbed the back of my head and pulled my face to his before kissing me. "Now let's stop all this gangsta shit. It ain't for us."

I looked into his eyes when our lips separated.

I can't believe how handsome he is. More than anything he's all mine. Our relationship is not like everybody else's but it works for us. We do a little bit of everything in the bedroom and it wasn't until I found him on that dating site that my dream came true.

Finally a man as wild as me.

Sometimes I get scared when I think about what would've happened if I never took a chance and logged on.

I may have never found him.

"So what we gonna do?" I snuggled closer and kissed his neck. "We got the entire house to ourselves and…" I kissed his lips. "I say we take advantage of the moment and fuck in every room in this apartment."

He grinned, lifted my chin slightly and planted another kiss on me. He loved kissing and so did I. Could do it all day especially if he was inside of my pussy. "So let me get this straight, we taking advantage of somebody else's pain? My man gets stabbed and now you want to fuck?" He asked playfully. "Because when I first got here all you wanted to do was talk 'bout gangsta shit."

I giggled. "It's sad but hey…" I straddled him. "We might as well enjoy each other. Otherwise Dandre's blood would be in vain." He was laughing so hard I could see all of his white teeth.

I loved that I could do that.

Make him laugh.

"Is that right?" He said.

"You know it is, Maceo."

I could feel him growing hard under my body. He was so stiff now that it was almost uncomfortable to sit on because it was poking at my inner thigh. "Go get the cord," He told me. "And go to your room. I gotta pee right quick."

My body went a little limp. "Can we leave that part out of it tonight?" I ran my finger down his jawline. "Please? Plus we don't know when everybody will come back and I don't want them to hear us."

He cocked his head to the side. "Come on, Paris. You know how I like it." He paused. "Do you got the cord or not?"

"Yes…I mean…I know how you like it, Maceo but—"

He lifted me up and sat me next to him. "When we first got together I told you how I liked to have sex."

He pointed at me. "You said you were with it too. Because I couldn't fuck with a woman that couldn't give me what I need in the bedroom. You know how many bitches wanna be with me? But I chose you because we the same. At least that's what you told me. Or are you running game?"

"I do want what you want, Maceo." I could feel my light skin reddening. "You know that."

"So then what's the problem?"

"The problem is that I wanted us to have a softer night for some reason." I smiled. "Come on, Maceo, if you wanna do it the other way later we can—"

He got up, walked into my room, grabbed his suitcase and wheeled it toward the door like he was about to leave. Eyes wide I jumped in front of him. "Hey...hey...don't do that...you just got here, Maceo."

"I been on planes all weekend," he said looking down at me. "If the truth be told I'm exhausted but I need a release and there's one way that happens. You and I both know it. Now are you gonna do it or not?"

I laid my head on his chest, touched his hand holding the handle of his suitcase and removed his grip from it softly. "I'll do whatever you want, Maceo.

Just please don't leave me tonight. I need you here. With me."

He squeezed my ass. "Then let's get to it ."

Fifteen minutes later we were in my room. He was sitting on the trunk bench, completely naked with his dick in his hand. I had one of his ties wrapped around his neck, which when pulled correctly based on the knot he made, tightened around his throat.

I couldn't find the cord so we used this instead.

When we were set up right he started jerking his dick and I tensed the tie to bring pressure around his throat. When it sounded like he was choking too much I released.

He seemed annoyed when he turned around and said, "FUCK YOU DOING? WHY YOU STOP?"

I jerked back a little thinking he was about to hit me even though he never had before. The tie dropped from my hand. "I thought I was doing it too hard and —"

"You know it's not too tight for me!" His eyes were red and he looked like a madman. I think he was more exhausted than he thought which when trying to cum this way meant a lot of work. "Now do it and don't stop until I give the signal. Aight?"

"Okay, Maceo, I got it." I scooted in the original position I was in before and grabbed the tie.

"Do you really?"

"Yes!"

"Then get at it." He turned around and we started it again. He jerked his dick and I tightened a little at a time. I used to like to be choked too but when I fell in love with him I realized sex was all I needed. I could leave this kind of thing alone but he couldn't live without it and I was not about to lose him.

I was tightening and tightening until I realized he wasn't jerking off anymore. His hands fell limp at his side and he seemed unconscious. Quickly I released the hold, knocked him to the floor and slapped him on the face. My eyes were bulging and my chest tightened because he didn't look good.

"MACEO, ARE YOU OKAY? MACEO, PLEASE! WAKE UP!" He moaned a little but gave no real sound. "OH MY GAWD! MACEO, PLEASE BE OKAY! I DIDN'T WANT TO DO THIS! I DIDN'T WANT TO DO THIS!"

His eyes were half opened but he didn't look like himself. His skin looked almost grey and his lips had no color at all. It was like I squeezed the life out of him.

"MACEO, YOU GOTTA SAY SOMETHING OR I'M GONNA CALL 911!" He was silent. "MACEO, I'M ABOUT TO CALL NOW!"

Finally he spoke in a soft tone. "Paris...I'm...I'm fine...Don't...don't call the police."

I lifted his head and put it in my lap. "Are you sure?"

"Yeah...guess I was too tired to...to...do it tonight. I should've listened to you." He tried to smile but it didn't work and his smile turned downward. "I guess you were right."

"You gonna stay here for the next few days."

"What about the..."

"Rules?" I said finishing his sentence. "I don't give a fuck about no rules. I'm not letting you out my sight."

When there was a knock at the door I helped him to my bed and put him under the covers. It was Barby and Kaden and they looked like a lot was on their minds.

The thing was, a lot was on my mind too.

CHAPTER SEVEN

BARBY

When Paris came out, dragging her feet, I realized Maceo was in her room and felt bad for knocking on her door. But I figured we didn't have a lot of time to talk about what happened at the hospital since Tabitha was at the grocery store. Basically I had to disturb her.

She could jump on Maceo's fine ass later.

She closed her bedroom door and walked toward us.

"Girl, I'm sorry but I gotta tell you what happened at the hospital," I said grabbing her hand and leading her to the sofa. I sat on one side of her and Kaden on the other.

"Aye, Paris, you aight?" Kaden asked. "You look like you fucked too hard in there." She giggled. "Everything cool?"

Paris glanced up at her and smiled. "Uh...yeah...I...I'm fine. I guess."

"You sure?" Kaden continued.

"The girl said she's fine so shut the fuck up," I said rolling my eyes. She acted like she wanted her to go back in the room or something.

"What she do this time?" Paris whispered, her hands looked limp in her lap. "Because yah look like you seen a ghost."

"First off she invited herself to take us to the hospital when we didn't need her ass," I said scooting closer. "Lakota had a car and we could've taken his but noooo. She had to be the one to take everybody to the hospital. She always including herself in anything that has to do with our niggas."

"But I thought he stabbed Dandre," Paris said. "Why would he take him to the hospital if they enemies now? That doesn't make sense, Barby."

"You know Lakota felt bad about what he did," Kaden said waving the air. "So trust us, we had a ride that didn't have to include Tabitha. But she wanted to be in the mix as usual."

"So I guess you starting to believe Barby too?" Paris said. "That Tabitha is up to no good?"

Kaden nodded. "Yep. After today I sure do."

"Anyway, so we get into the hospital and found out that even though Dandre lost a lot of blood he only had a cut on his finger," I said shaking my head. "All that blood for that small cut on his finger. It was crazy."

"So what happen?" Paris looked at her door and back at me. "I gotta tend to Maceo so you gotta get to the point."

"Girl, he'll be fine." I said. "The man looked like he was passed out when I saw him. Anyway, I told Tabitha she could go home and we could catch an Uber but she said no because she felt responsible."

Paris frowned. "Felt responsible for what? He not her man."

"Exactly!" Kaden yelled throwing her hands up in the air. "What she got to do with any of it?"

"She said if somebody died in this apartment, since the lease was in her name she would get in trouble!" I yelled. "But she's making a fucking excuse because we all on this lease. What she talking about? It's like she gotta be around Dandre for some reason!" I yelled.

"Hey, Barby, keep it down some." Paris said softly. "Maceo had a long night and I want him to get his rest. I keep telling you."

I looked at the door and back at her. "I'm sorry, girl, but I...I can't lose my nigga you know what I'm saying?" I got up and paced in front of the sofa before looking down at them. "He's the only man who really cares about me and wants me around. Dudes dump me after awhile and I don't know why. I'm a good woman, yah know that."

"He's a cool dude and all but you shouldn't be so pressed for a man," Kaden said as she got up, grabbed a bottle of red wine from the fridge and three glasses. "Especially if he fucking Tabitha like you say he is. You'll find another one don't worry."

"First off Tabitha gonna be mad as fuck when she come back and see you dug into the party stash," Paris said to Kaden. "And second weren't you the same person fighting for your nigga outside earlier, literally? So don't act like you high and mighty."

Kaden handed us each a glass, popped the cork and poured wine into our glasses. "You didn't hear what you think you heard outside, Paris. I wasn't fighting for anybody. Lakota and me had a problem but we working it out. Not much gonna change on our end so mind your business. We gonna be together as long as I'll have his ass." She sat the bottle down and flopped back on the sofa, almost spilling the wine everywhere.

"Are we getting off topic again?" I asked them. "We need to figure out what we gonna do 'bout her."

Paris frowned. "Wait, are you suggesting we leave just because Tabitha *might* be fucking your man?"

"Paris, please listen to this shit." I sat in between Kaden and her. "When we get into the hospital, the doctor was telling me everything that happened with Dandre's hand. I think he thought I stabbed him because he was telling me why the cut caused so much blood like he wanted me to feel guilty or something.

I sipped my wine. "Anyway, while I'm talking to him in the hallway, Dandre calls for Tabitha inside the room where he was being stitched by a nurse."

"So?" Paris shrugged. "What does that mean, Barby?"

"So I'm in the hallway looking like a fool and she's in the room with Dandre." I gulped all my wine. "And then...get this...he gives her some money."

Paris's eyes widened. "Wait, gave her some money? What you talking about?"

"I don't know why! That's what I'm trying to tell you. They have something going on and if she did it to me she'll do it to yah too. We shouldn't trust her ass."

Paris sighed and wiped her hand down her face. "So what you suggesting we do?"

I looked at Kaden who nodded. "We moving out."

"What? Why?" Paris yelled.

"Keep your voice down! Remember?" Kaden said. "Maceo is sleep."

"Yah know you can't leave right now." Paris said a little softer. "If you two roll out me and Tab can't afford the rent alone. She'll have to post it in the paper and then I'll be forced to live with new bitches."

"So come with us then," I said touching her leg. "Please? The three of us would be good in an apartment together." I looked at her and then Kaden. "Don't you think so?"

"So you're moving in together?" Paris paused. "When did you come up with this?"

"At the hospital, while she was busy keeping time with my man." I told her.

"Well when is this supposed to go down?" She asked me.

"You know the lease renewal is coming up so I figure we tell her after the party." I said. "So you in or not?"

She shook her head no. "Why can't you just ask her if she fucking Dandre first instead of jumping to conclusions?" Paris asked. "All of this shit could be innocent."

"Why would I do that? So Dandre can be mad at me again? Every time we get into a fight he tells me I'm being petty. He'll fuck around and leave me for her. I rather leave this apartment instead."

"Then I'm with, Kaden. Dump his ass."

"Look, the move is going down, Paris!" I said crossing my arms. "And because we fuck with you we wanted to tell you something else too."

"We taking the rent money out the bank for our new apartment." Kaden said.

"Wait, why you taking the rent money?" Paris yelled in a squeaky voice. "How the fuck are we gonna pay rent if yah got it?"

"We need a fresh start and some cash to go with it," I told her. "That's what I'm trying to say, this is going down with or without you. You might as well jump on board."

Paris stood up and laughed "I can't believe yah jumping to conclusions. If you ask me you being selfish."

"Did you know that Tabitha knew Maceo before you did?" I asked with a sly smile. "Did he tell you that? Because I bet he didn't."

Her eyebrows rose. "Wait, where you get that from?"

"He liked her back in the day," I continued. "Lakota told Dandre and I overheard them today at the hospital. When they knew we were listening they stopped talking but I overheard it already."

"So they were doing all that gossiping even though Lakota stabbed Dandre?" Paris asked. "Sounds pretty unbelievable to me."

"Yes!" Kaden said. "I keep telling you they good now."

"I wonder what else Maceo and Tabitha did that Maceo ain't telling you, Paris?"

She glared at me. "What you should be concerned with is whether or not Lakota not gonna kill Dandre's ass." She looked at Kaden. "Or vice versa. All this other shit is petty and I'm not going anywhere." Paris walked toward her bedroom, leaving us outside.

Kaden moved closer. "You think we pushed too hard?" She whispered. "Cuz I think lying to her about Maceo and the money may have been wrong."

"First of all what's done is done," I said. "Plus we had to find another way to get her onboard."

"Well that may not have worked," she said "She seemed mad. What we gonna do now?"

"I'm gonna stay on her hard. We gonna make her feel so uncomfortable to live here that she will jump to live with us."

"And if that don't work?"

"Kaden, you should know that if I don't get what I want nobody will be happy. Not her or anybody else."

CHAPTER EIGHT
BARBY

The maintenance man just left from fixing the window and I was prepping the chicken thighs for tomorrow's party for Tabitha. While seasoning them, my red locs were brushing against the meat. I was gonna put them in one single braid but something was on my mind and I didn't give a fuck if it was gross.

All I could see was Tabitha.

Every so often I'd look at her and wonder what my man saw in her. To me she wasn't all that. Yes, she was cute but her entire body was fake. I'm talking fake tits, fake ass and fake lips.

I can't stand her red ass!

What made me more annoyed was that she didn't seem to realize I didn't like her. I would even make little comments whenever she brought up Dandre's name to fuck with her but she just smiled, hugged me and called me crazy.

"Girl, we gonna have so much fun tomorrow!" Tabitha said excitedly as she chopped onions on the kitchen's counter. She turned around and looked at me and frowned. "Hey, put your locs up. They're on the food."

I knocked them toward my back and kept doing what I was doing. Salting the fuck outta the chicken. People would need a ton of water after eating these shits. "My bad." I rolled my eyes.

"So your friends coming over for our party?" She asked.

"You know my roomies are the only friends I have." It felt so gross talking to her but I needed to keep her off my trail until I convinced Paris to move with us tonight.

She smiled. "You know what, Barby, I think that's the way it should be." She shrugged. "Truth is you can't trust everybody. At least I can't."

She looked over her shoulder and smiled at me before dicing vegetables again. I think staying in the kitchen was her way of acting like she was never doing anything. Like she was too busy cooking to be trying to steal bitches' niggas from up under them.

I wasn't buying it.

"Outside of you guys the only person I talk to is my sister." Tabitha continued. "And I'm good on the rest of these chicks. Keep them away from me is my motto."

"You right about that." I rolled my eyes again. "On the you can't trust people part."

KNOCK. KNOCK. KNOCK.

Tabitha turned her head quickly and her long hair whipped over her shoulder. It was the only thing real on her by the way. "Can you get that for me, Barby?" she asked. "I don't want to smear onion juice all over the doorknob."

"Yeah, please don't do that gross shit," I rolled my eyes again.

"You so silly, Barby." She giggled. "That's why I fuck with you. You make me laugh."

UGHHHH! I CAN'T STAND HER! She really doesn't know I don't like her. Or maybe she does and doesn't care.

I wiped my hands on a strawberry red towel and opened the door. It was Chaviv, her boyfriend. Chaviv had to be about 6'3 or taller. He had really smooth light skin and soft brown hair. They looked so cute together which was why I can't understand why she was always up under my nigga. "Hey, Chaviv." I smiled, before stuffing my hands in my back pockets. "What's up?"

He gave me a quick kiss on the cheek. "Hey, B." He looked over my head. "Where Tab?"

"In the kitchen cooking for the party as usual. You know how she is boy. Come on in." I opened the door wider and he bopped inside like he had no cares in the world. But I was going to fuck up his peaceful situation.

"I know she thought I forgot her shit." He nodded and raised his hand with the bags. "But I got everything right here."

"Hey, bae," Tabitha said walking out of the kitchen, removing the bags from his hand and placing them on the counter. "At first I thought you weren't gonna make it until I remembered you always got me."

"I told you I was coming but you know shit is on my time." He winked. "The streets ain't punctual, baby girl. I can only get away after the money collected." He slapped her ass. "You know that."

Tabitha went through the bags slow at first, before speeding up. While looking inside one of them she frowned and said, "Chaviv, you forgot the ground beef! I need that for the cheese taco dip. See, I knew you would mess up! That's why I tried to call you today to remind you but you didn't answer the phone."

"Fuck," He ran his hand down his face. "I knew it was something. Sorry, bae."

"Can you please go back and get it for me?" She paused. "I'm almost ready for the meat and I don't have the time to go myself."

He sighed. "Aight, man, but you stressing me the fuck out 'bout this party shit. I know that. I be glad when this shit is over. Who the fuck have a party just 'cause they got a crib together? You ain't even charging niggas. They just eating and drinking on your dime. Dumb!"

"Can you please get my stuff?" She said rolling her eyes. "Let me worry about who paying in my house."

She seemed mad and I loved it.

"Man…aight," he stomped toward the door.

"I'll go with you," I said grabbing my keys. "I need a few things too. Might as well catch a ride."

"Good, maybe you can make sure he picks up the right stuff," Tabitha said before focusing back on the onions and green peppers on the counter.

Five minutes later I was in Chaviv's red pick up truck listening to 'Going Viral' by *Kodak Black* while wondering if I could trust him with what I was about to say.

"You can skip around on the songs if you want," he told me. "I got a lot of new shit on my playlist so its whatever's your pleasure."

"Nah, the music's okay, I like this one anyway." I moved my head a little so he could believe me before looking at him out the side of my eye. I wasn't in here for music. I was in here to fuck up Tabitha's shit. "So how long yah been together?"

He looked at me and back at the road. "I figure you talking 'bout my shawty."

"Yeah…"

"Long enough for a nigga to be loyal." He gripped the steering wheel as if I was about to come onto him and he was stopping me short. Chaviv need to go head with that shit. If I wanted to have him I could and he knew it. "She cool people though."

I smiled. "That's nice of you." I nodded. "To be loyal to somebody that…that…you know what, I'm not gonna do that." I shook my hand. "Dandre always talking 'bout I talk too much. So let me prove him wrong this time."

He chuckled. "Niggas say the same 'bout me but it ain't true. About I can't hold water."

"Yeah, I'm gonna leave it alone because I don't want no problems."

He frowned. "If you got something to say spit it out and stop with the games."

"It ain't my place. Plus Tabitha's my roommate and I don't want her mad at me. We do have to live together."

"If you feel that way why you talking then?" His jaw clenched. "I hate that shit."

"Chaviv, don't get mad at me because—"

"I'm a real nigga, B, and you might not be used to being in the company of a real nigga." He said cutting me off. "Not saying your dude ain't but we different. That means I ain't got time for the he say she say shit. Now if you gonna say something spit it out or get the fuck out my truck."

Suddenly saying anything felt dangerous. He was liable to snap and I didn't want it to be on me. I moved uneasily in his leather seat and it groaned. "I...I think your girl is fucking Dandre. I'm almost 90% sure."

Slowly my eyes rolled on to him to see his expression. "I just thought you should know that shit."

I could see him clench the steering wheel again. "My girl fucking Dandre? How you sound. As much as I be banging Tab's back out, what would she see in that dude? Plus when would she get the time? Nah, you got the facts smeared, shawty."

"I'm just saying what it is." I shrugged. "You don't have to believe me if you don't want."

"So if my broad fucking your dude, and you really believe that why you ain't step to him? Why you rapping to me about it?"

"Who said I didn't talk to Dandre?"

"Well where's the proof he stabbing my girl?" He asked.

I thought about this for a minute because I needed him to believe me. At the same time I didn't want him to do too much and my plan to get both of my roommates out blow up in my face. So I said, "I think I saw them kissing. They were real close and it didn't look or feel right to me. That's all I got for now."

He stopped his truck in the middle of the road. Cars beeped their horns and drove around us but not without throwing their middle fingers in the air and yelling.

He could care less because his eyes remained on me. "What you just say? About them kissing? You seen this with your own eyes?"

"Like I said, I can't be sure because it was in the hospital and so much was going on. I don't know if you heard but Dandre got stabbed last night."

"FUCK THAT NIGGA. I WANT TO KNOW 'BOUT MY BITCH."

I swallowed the lump in my throat. "I…I mean…he was getting stitched up and I walked out and I saw them together."

"This ain't adding up to me." He shook his head from left to right rapidly. "It don't feel right."

"I wasn't the only one who think they saw it, Chaviv. Kaden was there too and if you don't believe me you can ask her."

He rubbed his hand down his face. "So did she kiss the nigga or not? Because now you saying somebody else saw it but at first you weren't sure. Is it fact or fiction?"

"All I'm saying is to pay attention to your girl. That's it."

"Aye, how I know you ain't jealous?" He gritted on me. "You seem like the type anyway." He looked me up and down like I stunk. "Jumping into a nigga's truck and shit without an invitation. You know how thirsty that must have looked to her? But did she stop and say you couldn't go? Nah, she said to remind me to pick up what she wanted. That's cause she ain't insecure like you."

I swallowed the second lump in my throat. "See, now I got you upset, Chaviv, I—"

"I'm gonna find out for myself if Tabitha is doing whatever you claiming." He pointed at me. "But if I find out you lying you gonna be in a situation, B. I don't play with shit like this." He pointed downward. "It's best you know that. Dandre fucking my girl is disrespectful on all levels and he'd have to be dealt with too. If you loved the nigga you probably shoulda never told me."

My phone rang and I was happy because he was way too intense. I didn't spend a lot of time around him but now I think it was a mistake to even get him involved.

As a matter of fact I'm sure it was.

I placed my cell against my ear just as he pulled into traffic. "Hey, Kaden." I swallowed again before looking at Chaviv who was staring at me as if he wanted to tear me to pieces. "What's...what's up? I'm kind of busy right now."

"Girl, you gotta come back! Something wrong with Maceo!"

CHAPTER NINE
PARIS

MOMENTS EARLIER

I think I messed up. I think I really, really, messed up!

Maceo been acting crazy ever since I choked him last night. This morning when I woke up and asked him if he wanted breakfast, he just stared at the ceiling like I wasn't in the room. I tried to kiss him and he let me but he was still as stone like he was in a casket. If I didn't see his stomach going up and down I would think he was dead.

With him in the bed looking like a zombie I picked up my cell phone and called my best friend. She didn't come over much since I spent so much time with my roommates but she was always there when I needed her.

And I needed her now.

"Hey, Pooch...what you doing?" I sat on the floor across from the bed. From my view I could see him clearly and he was still lying down with his eyes

BY SHAY HUNTER

opened. "I...I miss you so much. When can I see you? Hopefully soon."

She giggled. "I'm not coming so don't ask."

I rolled my eyes and was happy to feel some other emotion for the moment instead of fear. "I wasn't asking you to come to the party tomorrow, Pooch so stop the nonsense."

She giggled. "Girl, please don't act like you haven't been working on me for weeks. I just wanted you to know that nothing will change. I'm going to see Drake anyway."

"Nope, it ain't about that. I realize you gonna do what you gonna do and that includes anything else but hanging with me and my roommates." I paused. "After my conversation with them recently I can't even blame you." I thought about Barby starting shit with Tabitha.

She laughed harder. "Good, just so you know I love you though."

"Even if I was arrested?"

"Wait...what?"

My eyes widened as my question replayed in my mind. "If something were to happen to me, would you come see me in jail? Or would you abandon me like you did with me living here?" I paused. "Because I need to know right now."

"Paris, you scaring me."

"Answer the question, Pooch!"

"I might not come over there but I see you every free chance you get. You know that. But where's the time? If you ain't with them chicks you with Maceo. So don't put that on me." She paused. "So yes, if you were locked up I would be there for you."

"Good to hear..."

"Now what happened? You finally buried one of your roommates? I'll help you tuck the body if you did." She giggled.

I laughed. "No, I wish it was that simple." To get my mind off of Maceo possibly dying I skipped the subject. "How you feel about my roommates? I mean really feel about them?"

"You mean Barby?"

When she said her name I remembered that she was the one she didn't like the most from a past conversation we had. "No, I'm talking about Tabitha."

"I'm gonna be real with you, if Tabitha was your only roommate I would visit you. She seems low-key and out the way. It's that Barby chick I can't trust. The last time I was there she was stirring up shit. I think something about her rent money being missing. I can't remember everything but I do remember her blaming yah and everything."

I forgot about that day until she said something. We spent a week trying to find her rent that she said was stolen only for Kaden to pay it. "Yeah...I remember that."

"I don't know how you forgot. She tried to fight you and everything." She paused. "And my hairdresser who used to do her hair said she will stir up shit anytime she can't get her way or feel threatened. I'm warning you to be careful. And look at her eyes when you talk to her."

"You always say that but why, Pooch?"

"Most people listen to what folks say but I pay attention to their actions and how they *look* at me when they say things. And her eyes are shifty."

"You got all that from the one time you hung around her?"

"With some bitches all you need is once."

I laughed and then Maceo started shaking violently on the bed and I lost reason. "Pooch...I...I gotta call you back." My voice trembled as I stood up.

"What's wrong, Paris? Are you feeling okay? You scaring me!" She said.

"I'll hit you back." I flung my phone down and ran over to Maceo who didn't look real. His body was vibrating so hard his teeth chattered. "Maceo, what's wrong? Talk to me! Say something!"

Instead of answering he started convulsing harder and foam oozed out the side of his mouth and toward the back of his head. Scared, I ran out of the bedroom where Kaden and Tabitha were in the kitchen getting ready for the party tomorrow.

"HELP!" I yelled out in to the apartment. "Something's wrong with Mace!" I dipped back into my room and now he was hanging off the bed shaking even harder. Tabitha and Kaden rushed on the other side of the bed and tried to help him up but he was moving so hard they couldn't control him.

"MACEO!" Kaden yelled grabbing his hand. "WHAT'S WRONG? SAY SOMETHING!"

"Did you call 911?" Tabitha asked, a little calmer than Kaden. "Because we have to do that!"

I didn't move.

I couldn't even talk.

My heart thumped hard and I felt like I was losing my mind.

"PARIS, DID YOU CALL 911?" Tabitha yelled grabbing my hand.

I blinked a few times. "No...I was scared," I admitted.

"Oh no, Paris!"

She left the room and from where I was on the bed I could see her about to pick up the phone but suddenly he stopped jerking. "HE'S FINE!" I yelled, just before she hit the numbers. "TABITHA, HE'S FINE! DON'T CALL THEM! HE HATES POLICE!"

I focused on Maceo again. He blinked a few times and wiped his mouth with his hand. "What's going on?" He asked me. "Why am I hanging off the side of the bed?" He positioned himself flat on the bed.

I was so happy he was talking I didn't know what to do. I lowered my body and hugged him tightly and cried on his chest. "Baby, you were having a seizure. Are you okay? How do you feel?"

He rubbed his temples. "My head hurts but I'm fine."

"I think we should still call 911, Paris," Tabitha suggested. "Just so they can check with him and see what's wrong. This doesn't look too good."

I heard the front door open and Chaviv and Barby walked into the room. "Is he okay?" Barby asked, with wide eyes.

"Man, you need anything?" Chaviv asked Maceo.

"I'm good, my dude." He said giving him some dap. "Just had a seizure I think. I'll be fine."

I looked at Chaviv and said, "You mind if I talk to my roomies alone?"

"No problem. I'm gonna make a run." He looked at Barby and then kissed Tabitha on the cheek. But it didn't seem loving like it had been in the past but Tabitha didn't seem to notice. "I'll be back." He walked out and closed the door.

I moved away from Maceo, to the corner of my room and they followed me. "Tab, I know the rules are that no boyfriends can stay over three nights straight but I don't want him going home right now. You saw how he was. He can't be alone like that."

"I'm fine, Paris," he said from across the room.

"No you not, Maceo. You just had a—"

Suddenly Kaden stomps out and slams the door shut. "What was that about?" I asked Tabitha and Barby about her behavior.

"I don't know but I'm gonna find out," Tabitha said.

I kissed Maceo on the forehead. "I'm gonna be right back."

"Okay. But don't make a fuss over me, Paris. And whatever you do don't call 911. I don't want them in my business. Please, bae."

"I won't." I nodded and Tabitha and me followed Kaden into her room where she was seated on the bed with her arms crossed tightly over her chest.

"Yah got some double standards in this house," Kaden said. "I know that shit."

I frowned. "What you talking about?" I asked. "What double standards?"

"It's okay for Maceo to stay here but yah didn't let Lakota stay that one time."

I looked at Tabitha and Barby. "First off Lakota wanted to *live* here," Barby said. "Maceo only staying a few days until he feels better. That's two totally different things."

Yeah, her nigga stayed broke and mine just wanted to feel better before living.

"I don't care what yah say. It's cause of you that Lakota left me. Had yah let him stay he wouldn't have gotten a new spot with a girl. This is so fucked up."

My eyebrows rose. "Wait, Lakota lives with another female?" I asked.

She frowned. "Yes, and I wonder why? Because yah wouldn't let him be here with me."

Tabitha sat next to her and put her hand on her back. She started rubbing it slowly. "I'm sorry that happened to you, Kaden. But we agreed on the rules when we rented this place so nobody would have to pay more just because a boyfriend lived in our apartment and used too much water, electricity or even food. We tried to keep things even."

Tabitha's phone rang and she took it from her pocket. First she looked at the screen, then at Barby before stuffing it back into her pocket.

"I'm sorry, Kaden but like I said we all agreed and we have to stick with the rules," Tabitha said.

Kaden rolled her eyes. "All I know is yah still got your niggas. Meanwhile my relationship is fucked up."

She stood up. "And I'ma leave it at that." She left the room.

Tabitha walked up to me. "Maceo can stay for a couple of days, but after that he has to go." She sighed. "I'm really sorry, Paris. I hated seeing him like that but Kaden is right." She left the room and then the apartment.

CHAPTER TEN

BARBY

When Tabitha walked out I went to my room and I had my eyes planted on her from the window the whole time.

Where was that bitch going and who was on the phone?

One minute she was laying down the law as usual and the next she was gone. Well I didn't trust that chick so I left Kaden's room and went to my own so that I could have a better view outside of the apartment building. The way she looked when her phone beeped gave me the creeps. Maybe Chaviv told her to come outside to tell her what I said to him in his truck.

If she wanted to fight me because of it I would be ready.

I pushed the curtains to the side and gazed out the window. From where I was I could see Tabitha walking to Dandre's car and my jaw dropped. He didn't even hit me to tell me he was here and now she meeting him in his car?

BY SHAY HUNTER

I paced the room. My temples throbbed and my head hurt. This was fucked up on so many levels. Everything in me said to go outside and to confront her but Dandre and I had been in so many arguments over me allegedly blowing things out of proportion.

What could I do?

I turned around and yelled, "PARIS AND KADEN! COME TO MY ROOM QUICK! NOW!"

Within seconds they rushed inside. "Look out the window." I pointed.

Paris frowned and pushed the curtain aside just as Tabitha was getting into my man's car. When the car door was closed I said as calmly as I could, with sweat rolling down the sides of my face, "Now yah believe me?" I wiped it away. "Now do you see what I'm saying?"

Paris released the curtain and stared at me like I was a homeless person. I could feel how sorry for me she felt.

Kaden remained tight lipped.

"I'm not gonna lie, that didn't look right," Paris admitted. "I'm just not understanding what got into her all of a sudden. If somebody did this to Chaviv she would lose her mind!"

I guess she was finally coming over to my side because her eyes darted around as if she was trying to think of what else to say.

"Now when I say that she's janky as fuck you'll realize I'm not talking out the side of my neck," I said. "Now maybe you'll see why I go off so much around here." I paused. "I know it may seem like I just don't like her, or like I'm jealous for whatever reason but that's not the case. This girl foul!"

"This is dumb," Kaden said. "If you not gonna step to her about this shit I am." She was about to walk out when I grabbed her arm. "What? You should be going with me not stopping me."

"Don't do that," I said. "Because I'm not gonna be here long. Neither are you. Remember?"

She yanked away from me.

"If you gonna let this shit slide then I'm going to my own room," Kaden said with a major attitude.

"What's really wrong with you?" I asked. "Because you can't be mad at us about what Tabitha said. And I know you not mad at Paris because Maceo is staying and Lakota couldn't live here."

She flopped on the bed and started crying. "He's done with me. He made an excuse as to why he didn't want to be with me after he begged me to talk to Dandre for him."

My eyes widened. "Begged you to talk to Dandre?" I moved next to her.

"Yes...he was afraid some heat would come back on him for stabbing Dandre. He thought the streets would be after him so I talked to Dandre for him and told him Lakota didn't mean nothing by it. I begged him not to take things far."

"Dandre said you talked to him," I said. "But just so you know, Dandre already let that shit go the moment it happened. He said it was street shit and he wasn't worrying about it so I'm not either."

"The shit ain't over," Paris said. "I don't care what Dandre saying. If you love your nigga tell him to be careful, Kaden."

I frowned. "What you know about all that?" I asked Paris.

She placed her hands on her hips. "Enough."

I focused back on Kaden who was an emotional mess. "I don't know about the street stuff but I just want him back yah. I can't not be with Lakota. I can't have some other girl calling him daddy. What am I going to do?" She held her chest. "It hurts so bad."

I can't believe this was the same chick last night telling me to stop being so pressed over niggas while holding a glass of wine. It's mighty funny that the tides have turned.

"If you don't get him back you'll get a new nigga," I assured her. "When we get a place of our own."

"Barby's right, Kaden," Paris said. "If Lakota wants to beef with you it's his loss not yours." She walked up to her and played with the portion of her hair she hadn't finished braiding. "Now when you gonna let me get back into this?"

"Tonight if you wanna."

Paris smiled and then frowned. "If I can get the time, with Maceo being sick and all."

Kaden looked at Paris. "And I want you to know I'm not beefing with Maceo. I just hate how Lakota wasn't even considered for living here for a few days when he got put out of his crib. It wasn't even up for discussion and he throws that up in my face all the time. That I have no clout in my own apartment."

"Exactly, and you notice who made all the rules," I said with raised eyebrows.

"Tabitha," we all said together.

"For some reason, just leaving and stealing the rent money ain't enough for me no more," Kaden nodded with an evil look in her eyes. "I think we should do something else. Something she can feel."

My eyes brightened. "Like what?"

"What if we beat her ass too?" Kaden suggested. "We should lure her into one of the rooms and fuck her up. We would have to be packed already so we can roll after but still. What you think?"

I clapped once. "I love that shit!"

Everybody but Paris seemed to be down with the idea.

"Me too," Kaden said through clenched teeth before walking over to the window. "Look at her disrespecting hard. I mean she's still in the car with Dandre. Posted all up like they legit with this shit."

Paris shook her head. "I can't believe you letting it go down, Barby. I would be outside swinging on both of them by now. You way calmer than me that's for sure."

"Yeah, what is the real reason you don't want to go with the hands?" Kaden asked. "You scared she may get the best of you or something? I can help you fight her if you want."

"It ain't that." I sighed and slapped my long locs away so that they hung down my back. "The last time I tried to approach Dandre about something. It was a girl I saw him talking to at a BARBEQUE he didn't invite me to one day." I wiped the tears away. "Well I got the address from one of his friends and went anyway. When I got there I saw him with this chick and went off. Like, nobody could hold me. My arms were flinging everywhere. I knocked over one of the grills, tossed food on the floor and tried to snatch the hair off the chicks' head." I paused. "It was a very bad night."

"What ended up happening?" Paris asked.

"I found out it was a relative. One of his aunts I never met. To this day his mother doesn't talk to me for what I did to her sister." I shrugged. "A lot of situations happened like that and when the smoke clears I'm always in the wrong. Dandre said the next time I didn't trust him he would cut me off for good. That was months ago." My eyes lowered. "I'm smarter now."

Paris walked up to me. "But Tabitha's not kin to him, Barby. And if you wanna know if she's fucking your man you gotta step to her like a woman."

I looked at her for a moment and thought about what she was saying. My heart knew she was speaking truth but now things had escalated beyond that. My plan was to move out of this apartment with my nigga in tact and destroy her life, not mine.

I pushed her away from me. "We need an answer, Paris."

"About what?" She frowned.

"You haven't told us what you gonna do." I crossed my arms over my chest. "About moving with us."

"Yes I did. I told you I haven't made a decision yet."

"Nah, you didn't say nothing," I said inching closer. "That's what's bothering me. You know all of our business but we don't know what you thinking."

"I did say something the other day. I said I like staying here but—"

Kaden walked up to her. "You're either with us or you're not." She cracked her knuckles. "Because if you aren't with us you can get it too."

"You threatening me?"

"Take it how you want, pretty girl."

Paris backed up to the wall and from where she stood I could see out the window. A smile spread across my face when I saw Chaviv pulling up while she was sitting in my nigga's car.

"Kaden, come over here right quick!" Kaden approached us and Paris turned around to see what I was looking at out the window. "I tried to put him on that his bitch was a freak earlier today and he wouldn't listen." I shook my head when I saw Chaviv getting out of his car to approach Dandre's. "Bet he listening now."

"You did what?" Paris yelled, a frown on her face.

"You heard me!"

"Why would you do that?" She continued. "You don't even have any facts."

"Is that not enough?" I pointed at the window.

"I don't know what that's about. But I do know Tabitha is not like that." She paused. "Plus what you think Chaviv gonna do if he really believed they fucking? He ain't one of them keep it light dudes. He may be liable to hurt both of them. Maybe you should've thought about that before you did that shit!" She stormed out.

CHAPTER ELEVEN

TABITHA

MOMENTS EARLIER

I rushed into Dandre's car and slammed the door. Once inside I looked at the window to make sure my roommates weren't looking. I thought I saw the curtain close but I couldn't be sure.

This situation between me and Dandre was getting way out of control.

Taking a deep breath I turned to face him. "You gonna have to be careful, Dandre." My breaths were still heavy from running to his car. "Barby might start suspecting something if you keep asking to see me alone. Talking to me in the house is one thing. Texting me and telling me to come out front is different."

"I know this was too much but I ain't know how else to do it." He shrugged. "I got a lot of shit on my plate and needed to rap to you about it. I mean, sorry if I overstepped."

I was so irritated it was hard to hide. "Well what's so important, Dandre?" I looked behind me at Barby's window again before facing him. Nobody seemed to be looking out. "Because as you know this is highly inappropriate."

"Man, I'm sorry. I fuck up even when I'm not trying," he raised a beer bottle to his mouth that I didn't know he had and gulped most of it. I figured he'd been drinking because of his mood and the way he texted me telling me to come outside. It was something he'd never done in the past.

I looked at his bandaged hand. "So how your finger feel?"

He looked down at it and moved it a little. "This ain't about nothing. I'm gonna handle this situation for real."

I nodded. "So what you want with me, Dandre? You gotta hurry up because I feel like something is about to happen."

"I been having second thoughts on the situation." He paused. "I'm talking about me and Barby getting married and shit."

I turned toward him, my eyes widened and I breathed heavily. "Please don't play like that, Dandre. Don't tell me you not gonna propose to that girl."

"I wouldn't fuck around like this. It ain't a game. I'm not feeling the whole thing no—"

"But why would you change your mind?" I asked interrupting him. "You already got the ring! Why put it off now?" I could feel my heart beating as the responsibility weighed on my shoulders for him changing his mind. "What you don't like her no more? Did yah have a fight?"

"Nah, it's more than that."

"Well what is it?" His silence was irritating and it had me wanting to walk away. There was nothing to stop somebody from seeing us in the car together and there would be no explaining it away. Part of me wanted to tell him to pull up the block, away from my building, but I didn't want to be around him too long. "Say something and stop sitting over there looking crazy, Dandre."

"Okay, maybe I'm not feeling her," he shrugged. "Sometimes when I look at her I'm like, yeah she'll do, but then I realize there's something about her I don't like. Or a lot of shit about her I don't like. I can't put my finger on it."

I ran my hand down my face. "You sure this not 'bout something else?" I paused. "Like the beef with

Lakota, because I know you. You don't do something so major like a proposal and then change your mind without a reason."

He waved the air. "Like I said, I'ma deal with that Lakota shit in my own way. On my own time."

"Dandre..."

"I'm serious." He took another sip of beer. "I thought about it and I wasn't 'bout to let street shit get out of hand right now. Have you even seen him? Because I been looking for him."

I didn't feel like being in the mix of the streets. "You know what, this is dumb." I moved to get out of the car and he stopped me. "Listen...you right, Tabitha."

I flopped in the seat and looked at him. "Finally the truth."

"I gotta strike back at Lakota but I gotta be smart. If I do something and he retaliates against my girl I'm going off, Tabitha. Like you've never seen me like that but—"

I shook my head, closed my eyes and opened them again. "I'm confused, why you taking her ring back again? You all over the place out here."

"Because I don't want her mixed in."

"If you love her, Dandre, like you say you do, please don't do that. I'm begging you not to." I paused. "You have to think of —"

"Hold up...ain't that Chaviv's truck?" He asked squinting in front of him.

"Oh my gawd! This is what I was talking about. This is what I didn't want to happen, Dandre. Bet he think something is up between us." I watched him park, get out and approach. "Let me go speak to him for a second."

Instead of coming to my side Chaviv knocked on Dandre's side of the car. The glare he gave him could chill ice. Dandre rolled down the window and they dapped each other softly.

"What's going on?" Chaviv asked looking at me and then Dandre. "Am I missing something? Yah having the party early in this bitch?"

"Hey, baby..." I said with a nervous smile. "I was...I was..."

"I asked what's going on, Tabitha?" He said through clenched teeth. "You making me feel some kind of way and you know what that means. For everybody involved."

Of course I did. It meant somebody had to die.

I looked at Dandre. "Tell him…so he'll know."

"But you said Chaviv can't hold water," He responded.

I almost threw up in my mouth. I told him that weeks ago, not because he was a blabbermouth. That couldn't be further away from his personality. It was just that he was so laid back that he forgot about things that were told to him in confidence especially while smoking weed. His laid back attitude meant any secret was threatened during regular conversation.

"Hold up, what you mean I can't hold water?" Chaviv frowned. "That ain't true."

"Just show him the ring," I encouraged. "He's good, Dandre. He ain't gonna tell Barby and that way he'll know what's going on. Otherwise…"

Dandre was mad but he opened the glove compartment, slammed it shut and showed him the ring. "I'm proposing to Barby at the party tomorrow."

Chaviv grinned at the diamond and gave him some dap. Dandre put it up and Chaviv's entire expression was lightened and he looked relieved. "Congrats, my nigga. That's a good look for you. Because Barby was feeling some—"

He stopped in mid sentence. "Barby was what, bae?" I asked him. "What were you about to say?"

"Nothing...but what ya'll talking about now?" Chaviv continued. "Seems like you already made the decision. What you want with my girl now?" His tone was light but his words were serious.

"He was getting my advice on how to give her the ring, that's all." I shrugged. "He thought before everybody got to the party was good but then changed his mind. He thinking about taking her outside and proposing."

Chaviv nodded and knocked on top of the hood. "Well let's go inside before somebody see yah out here and be thinking some other shit. You know how chicks are in this neighborhood."

"You right." Dandre said.

I got out, closed the door and walked over to Chaviv, away from Dandre's car. He picked me up in a big embrace before planting a kiss on my face. "I like him, Tabitha. He cool people, but I don't want you spending alone time with another nigga. I feel like I shouldn't have to tell you this but it's obvious I do. Be careful."

I couldn't help but grin. "Wait, do I detect a little jealousy? You always act like you could care less."

"Keep fucking with me and you'll see *and* feel how much I care."

I smiled. "You know it's not like that with me. I would never do that to you."

"It ain't about that, it's about respect. You spoken for so that mean knowing how to carry yourself."

"I carry myself like a lady."

"Don't just carry yourself like a lady." He pulled me closer. "Carry yourself like *My* lady. There's a difference." He paused. "Be careful on what you do because people may be watching too."

I frowned a little. "Wait, you telling me something I need to know? Is one of the fake bitches around here talking shit? Because for real the only women I trust are my roommates."

He shook his head. "Like I said, no more side convos with dude, aight?"

I kissed him again and smiled. "I'm not gonna lie, jealousy looks good on you."

"And this dick gonna look good on you in a minute when I'm banging that back out." He slapped my ass and I giggled. "When it's on them lips."

"What we waiting on nigga?" He picked me up and carried me in the building. I saw Dandre walking behind us, with a glare on his face.

CHAPTER TWELVE

KADEN

We were in Barby's room staring out the window. Basically we watched what looked like Tabitha getting herself outta a tight situation between Chaviv and Dandre. I don't know what she said but it went from Chaviv's crazy ass knocking on Dandre's window to her getting carried in to the building by him.

When they disappeared I turned toward Barby and said, "The girl is good. Say what you want but if she got outta that something has to be magic about her."

Barby looked relieved that Chaviv didn't kill Dandre. I guess what Paris said stuck to her.

"Maceo's still sleep." Paris said walking back into the room. She looked at Barby and then me. "Anything happen outside? Is Dandre okay?"

I approached her. "Nope, things are calm for now." I exhaled. "So you gonna finish my hair tonight?" I fingered the section that was left. "Because I'm in a better mood now and need my shit done.

"Yeah, I can do it," Paris shrugged. "But what changed all of a sudden? Why you smiling?"

Barby just listened.

"Because when we beat this bitch's ass tomorrow, it will bring a smile to my face." I shook my head. "After seeing that shit outside, with her getting in Dandre's car, Barby went way past disrespect." I looked at Paris. "And after seeing that you have to be with us now."

She sighed. "I am kinda thinking moving with yah but I'm not about to be threatened when—"

"You so fucking chicken!" I said. "I can't even be mad because—" When my phone rang and I looked down and saw it was Lakota calling suddenly I couldn't remember what we were talking about. I don't even think I cared. "I'm going to my room, I'll be back."

"I thought we were having a conversation?" Paris said sarcastically.

"Girl, I be back! Just wait!" I ran to my room, closed my door and answered. "Lakota...how are you...I mean...what you doing?"

"How come I been calling and couldn't get you? Yesterday you had all the convo for me and now you mute! What's up with that, Kaden? You don't want me hitting you no more? Because I won't if that's how you feel."

My eyes widened. "Wait...when did you call? Cause I swear on everything I didn't get it."

"Does it matter? You ain't answer."

"Lakota, why you doing this to me? Why you telling me you don't love me and then...and then you call with all this? I can't take this up and down stuff with you. The mental games are killing me."

"I never said I didn't love you, Kaden. I said I couldn't be with you. Stop taking everything to heart."

My nose wrinkled and felt tingly. I was trying not to cry but it was hard every time he opened his mouth. "But I want to be with you! I want to hold you! I want to love you and I'm willing to do whatever I can to make that happen."

"You can't do anything but let shit be right now. Your problem is you try to force too much. Some shit just gotta work itself out on it's own time. I say that to you repeatedly. That's why you not ready to be my woman. You don't think big."

I felt like a balloon, which had been poked with a pin. "You right. I guess."

I heard him blow something and figured he was smoking. "Is Dandre over there? The streets saying they don't know where he is. And he ain't been answering my calls."

My eyebrows rose. "Why you asking about Dandre? I thought everything was cool."

"Again with the questions."

I rolled my eyes. "I saw him earlier but I think he left." I lied because I still didn't know what was happening with them and I didn't want to be involved in whatever beef they had going. I thought it was squashed but the way Paris was talking earlier I couldn't be sure.

"Well I'm coming over later."

The moment he said that I could hear Dandre in the living room laughing with Barby. I wanted nothing more than to see him. Then to lay my nose close to his neck and inhale. Then to feel his fingers along my back before somehow finding their way to my pussy. But if I invited him over I didn't want him fighting with Dandre.

"Kaden, are you there?"

"Uh...yeah." I cleared my throat.

"Can I stab through for a second? Just to kick it with you?"

I heard Dandre and Barby get louder and figured Dandre might be staying. "Lakota, can I come to your house? That way we can have a little more privacy?"

"Nah, you know you can't do that."

"Why?"

"Because I live with a girl, Kaden. Stop faking dumb."

I felt gut punched when I was reminded. That quickly when he asked to be with me I was taken to the time where it was just he and I. "Oh, I forgot. Sorry about that."

He laughed. "You trying to fuck or not, Kaden?"

What the fuck?

Gross!

I hung up on him. I don't even know why. For a second my fingers hovered over my phone as I considered calling him back. Instead, surprisingly, he called me. "So you hanging up on niggas now? That's your thing? I thought you loved me."

I smiled that finally he reached out to me first. Usually I was calling him and begging to be back together. "I'm sorry, I just…"

"I may have came at you wrong but if we ever gonna get back the only way it will work is if we spend time together. I mean, if you saying you don't want me no more then say it. I'll go on with my life and leave yours alone."

I knew he was fucking with my mind but how could I make him stop? I loved him too much. "You right…"

"So can I come over or not? I'm tired of asking you."

"Yeah, I have to make a few stops so I'll be home in a couple hours."

"Good, I'll see you at midnight. We have some more things to talk about." He hung up just as Paris knocked on my bedroom door. I needed to find a way to get Dandre out of here before Lakota came by so I didn't feel like company. I needed to think.

But the moment I opened the door Paris went in. "I don't care what we gotta do I'm down!" she said.

"I was just about to ask you to do my hair. Me and Lakota hooking up tonight. But what's wrong?"

She pushed past me and I closed the door. "So I walk into my room after talking to Barby when guess who I see coming out of my bedroom? Tabitha's ass?"

My eyes widened and my jaw hung. "Fuck you talking 'bout? What she doing in there? Maceo sick so I know he can't be keeping company."

"That's just what I said!" Tears rolled down her face as she got louder and wiped them away. "But he was up, smiling and shit. I'm ready to get out of this apartment. I don't fuck around when it comes to Maceo, you know that."

A grin formed on my face but I tried to contain my pleasure. "So does that mean you with us? Moving with us and everything?"

"If I could leave tonight, Kaden I would. That's on everything I love."

I shook my head. "This bitch think just cuz she was in this apartment first she can do anything she wants but nah."

Barby busted into the room and came up to us. "What happened? I saw how mad you were a minute ago." She looked at me and then Paris. "Well? Somebody say something!"

I smiled at her. "All you need to know is that Paris is down with us. Finally!"

Barby smiled sinisterly.

CHAPTER THIRTEEN
PARIS

I walked into the kitchen while Tabitha was making pizza for everyone for dinner. I remembered when I first got here I thought she was so cool because she cooked every night. Now I'm sure it's just a way to manipulate us. We're so used to her cooking that whenever she doesn't I secretly get an attitude. It's like I'm expecting it and I depend on her.

It was all about control with that girl.

Now I'm sure.

"Hey, Paris," she smiled after putting the last pepperoni on the pie. "How's Maceo?"

"He's fine," I walked up to the fridge and grabbed a beer. "Did he say anything when you talked to him?" I took a large gulp and swallowed.

"I didn't talk to him." She wiped her hands on her towel. "Except when he was having a seizure but I don't think he heard me. I don't think he heard any of us. You remember right?"

My eyebrows rose. "What you mean you didn't talk to him?" I sat my beer on the counter. "I saw you coming out of my room a little while ago."

"Oh, I was just checking to make sure your window was closed because the apartment wasn't getting warm." She giggled and clapped her hands together. "Girl, I thought you were crazy at first asking if I talked to Maceo. I forgot he was looking at me."

"The window open?"

"Yeah, when I went into Tabitha's room earlier hers was open and I was checking all of them to make sure shit was cool. You know the bill be high if we don't watch it an nobody likes to pay extra electricity around here."

I thought about what she was saying for a second but wasn't sure if she was being honest. We were looking out Barby's window all day so and I do know Tabitha is big on keeping the bill down. Everything seems so cloudy now. Barby and Kaden been feeding me hate for the past couple of days and I don't know what's true.

"Oh, I thought you were talking to him." I picked the beer up again and gulped half of it down. My eyes remained on her the entire time.

She giggled. "Girl, how could I talk to him anyway? He was knocked out."

She still lying! I saw him up smiling at her.

Tabitha's expression grew serious. "What's going on with him? He's been in the room all day. Has he been sick for long? Like with the seizures?"

"Not real long but—"

"I'm gonna tell you like I told Kaden, we can't have him here forever, Paris," she said cutting me off. "Niggas always use more energy than females and its unfair to everybody else. You saw how Kaden acted when I told her Maceo was staying."

"I never told you this, since you were here before us, but I think it's wrong that our boyfriends can't stay over longer than a couple of days." I paused. "We all grown, Tabitha and there should be a little more leniency around here. Don't you think? Plus I—"

"The lease is up on Monday, Paris." She wiped her hands on the towel over her shoulder. "If you and the girls wanna revisit boyfriends, maybe even pay more anytime our boyfriends stay longer than a week I'm okay with it." She paused. "But for now it's a no go. I hate to be the one to enforce the law but it has to be me since I brought us all together. I hope you understand."

THE ONE YOU SHOULDN'T TRUST   123

"It doesn't have to be that serious. With the meeting and all."

"But I think it does though. Lately it's been the same thing with yah, wanting your men to stay over longer than what we agreed on. I'm just tired of talking about it really."

My eyebrows rose. She never came at me like this before. I also noticed that to be twenty-four she acted mature. Everything with her seemed planned and old but her look and style.

"Whatever you say," I walked over to the counter. "But can you listen out for Maceo for me? I have to make a run right quick."

"You know I'm in here," she smiled. "Waiting on Chaviv to come back as usual. With his late ass."

I giggled and when I turned around rolled my eyes. All I knew was Maceo was up and she was a liar. And liars couldn't be trusted.

I knew Chaviv was probably over Moonday's house down the street because he hustled with him in

BY SHAY HUNTER

Southeast. Luckily Moonday was my cousin so my coming over didn't seem odd. The moment I pulled up I saw Chaviv's truck and tried to hide my pleasure because he was just the person I was looking for. Barby went to him earlier and I had intentions on supporting her claims.

Now I didn't trust Tabitha and I had plans to do something about it, like mess up her situation.

"Hey, cuz, what you doing here?" Moonday asked before gripping me into a tight hug. He was a big dude who wore his weight well. "I hit you the other day for my cookout but..."

"I know," I said. "Maceo had just gotten back in town and I wanted to spend time with him. You know how it is..."

"Yeah, as long as you don't cancel again. My friends starting to think I ain't got no cousin called Paris." He smiled. "So how Maceo doing?" he paused. "A friend of mine said he ain't been answering his phone the past couple of days."

"A friend of yours?" I asked with raised brows.

"It's not like that."

I scratched my scalp. "Is it a guy or girl?"

"Come on, cuz," he waved the air. "I ain't never know you to be sensitive. If I can't talk to you like family you got to get on from around here with all that. I don't need the drama."

"Nigga, stop fucking around and tell me the truth! Or are you holding a nigga who ain't blood over me?"

"Okay, it's a chick but it's not like that." He pointed at me. "They play brother and sister. Been knowing each other for as long as you and me. Trust me when I say it wasn't like that."

Now I was real angry. Whoever this chick was if they knew each other that long it meant they had a bond. "Moon, you know what, I'm not here for all that anyway." I looked around and over his shoulder. "Where's Chaviv?"

Soon as I asked for him he came outside and I could tell he was about to go because he had his keys in his hand. He opened the screen door and looked down at me. "Hey, Paris," he frowned. "Is Maceo okay? I was just thinking about that situation a second ago."

"Yeah, he cool, but can I rap to you for a minute?"

He looked at my cousin and shrugged. "Yeah, come on. I don't see why not."

"I'll get up with you later, Moon," I said after they gave each other dap.

Moon nodded and we walked to Chaviv's truck and got inside. When the door was closed he leaned back and said, "So what's on your mind?"

"I want to talk to you about, Tabitha." He chuckled hard and shook his head. "Fuck so funny?"

"Nah, it's nothing really. I just don't understand what she did to get yah so heated in that crib. First Barby and now you? Come on, man. I ain't no sounding board for everything Tabitha. She a grown woman. You got a grievance take it to her because I'm sure she would do the same."

I frowned. "So you okay that your girl a whore?"

He glared at me. "Watch it."

"It ain't about watching it. What it's about is that she not in line and in this moment you don't seem to care. I thought you loved her!"

He positioned his body so that he was looking into my eyes. Then he stared over my shoulder at Moonday who was on the porch drinking beer and laughing with a group of niggas.

"The only reason I haven't smacked the shit outta you is because you my man's cousin. But lets be clear, you not gonna get another chance to come at me like that again. I promise you that."

"Chaviv —"

"Chaviv, shit. Now unless you got proof I'm not trying to hear this shit all night. Cause I'm tired of you and your people coming to me with drama. Fuck I look like? Your bestie?" He asked sarcastically.

Tabitha had him right where she wanted him.

I nodded and grabbed my purse. "All I'm gonna say is be careful when you kiss them lips because they probably been around Dandre's dick." I pushed the truck door open before he could kill me and stomped away.

CHAPTER FOURTEEN
KADEN

I don't know where Paris went but when she returned she started braiding my hair tight as shit, like she had an attitude or something. She kept asking me what was the plan for tomorrow and she kept talking around herself.

The only thing I was sure of was that we were all in on the plan to fuck Tabitha up the next day and then get our own place. I don't think any of us thought much beyond that because we all had bad credit.

When my cell phone rang I smiled when I saw its Lakota again. "Who got you acting all silly?" Paris asked. "One minute you in emotional pain and the next you cheesing like shit."

"It's Lakota..."

"Yah back together?" She grinned and then frowned. She was mad at somebody. "If so when this happen?"

"Shhh..." I placed a finger over my lip and answered the call. "Hey, Lakota. Still coming over tonight right?" I figured the coast was clear since Dandre wasn't here. At least I hoped not.

"Yeah, but let me speak to Tabitha right quick."

I looked at the phone and placed it back on my ear. "Speak to Tabitha right quick? Why?"

Paris whispered, *"What the fuck he want to speak to her for?"*

"Please don't start tripping, Kaden. If I wanted you to know I would've said it. Now just put her on the phone."

I shook my head and stood up. "Where you going girl?" Paris asked. "Because I'm not gonna be on your hair all night. You gonna fuck around and have the same hairstyle for the party tomorrow."

I didn't even respond or care. Instead I stomped out and into the kitchen where Tabitha was taking one of the pizzas from the oven. I felt like throwing it on the floor, cheese part down. "Tab, it's the phone." My arm was out stiff with the screen to the iPhone in her direction.

She looked at it and then my eyes. "Who that, girl?"

"Lakota."

"Lakota?" She giggled. "What he want with me?"

"That's what I'm trying to figure out."

She shrugged and took the phone. "Hey, Lakota." She paused and giggled hard. "Oh...hey! Yeah, I know. I know. Yeah, you so right. Why you think I did it? Because I knew better." She laughed again and placed another pizza with sausage and mushrooms in the oven. "You better not or you gonna get in trouble..."

Here this chick was having a full fledge conversation with my boyfriend and nobody bothered to tell me what the topic was. Normally if you talking to a bitch's man you turn around and involve them every so often. But she not doing any of it. It's like I don't exist and she doesn't care. She was changing over night.

It took everything in my power not to hit her in the back of the head with one of these pans.

"Okay, I will," She said. "Talk to you later." She handed me back the phone.

"Well?" I asked.

"Well what?"

"What did he want?"

She waved the air. "Nothing for you to worry about."

She had me fucked up because I was nothing like Barby. I was gonna ask about mine.

"Tabitha, I'm not trying to be funny but I'm not cool with that. I'd appreciate if you told me what it was about so I can put anything funny out my mind."

She frowned. "Wait, you think I want Lakota?"

"No! I mean...I...I mean...I just wanna know what yah talking about."

"I wasn't talking to Lakota, Kaden. He was in the liquor store and my sister was in there and he gave the phone to her. She was the one I was talking too." She smiled. "Don't ever think of me in that way because you'll be wrong, Kaden. Why everybody acting so crazy around here lately? Keep it light. We're about to celebrate one year living together tomorrow."

I swallowed the lump in my throat. "Sorry."

"It's okay." She smiled again. "Is Barby and Paris here?"

"I think so."

"Well tell them to—"

Before Tabitha could finish her sentence Barby walked up to me and tapped me on the shoulder. "Let me holla at you for a minute outside."

"Why?" I asked. "We have our own rooms."

She looked at Tabitha who didn't seem to notice because she was focusing on the food and then she looked back at me. "It's important and private," she whispered.

"Aight," I said softly. Clearing my throat I said, "Tab, me and Barb stepping outside right quick. We be back."

"Well don't be out long, the pizza gonna get cold!" She said with a smile.

That bitch strange for sure.

When we were in front of the building Barby pulled me closer and said, "Do you remember that weed edible business we tried to open?"

I laughed. "Yeah, it was only last year plus the sign taking up space in the living room. Why you asking anyway?"

"I just looked at our bank account that we opened to pay rent and found out we're still paying for the insurance automatic deduction each month. Well, Tab been paying the extra amount but still."

I was still angry about Tabitha talking to Lakota or her sister so for real I wasn't interested in whatever she was saying. Was Tabitha being honest about talking to her sister? Barby fucked up my head so much I couldn't be sure. So truthfully I wanted her to get on with it. "And? Why does that matter?"

"Like you know we had to get the life insurance policy on each other before we got a license for the business. Tabitha's lawyer told us that remember? When we were in his office? Well anyway it's still in place even though the business didn't take off."

"What does that mean, Barby?"

"It means that if one of us dies it's one hundred thousand dollars cash. So, if Tabitha dies its one hundred thousand dollars."

Now she had my attention. "So wait what you saying?"

"I hate her, Kaden. A lot." She moved closer so that only I could hear her. I also felt her hot breath on my nose. "And the more I think about it the more I realize the world would be better off without her."

"But murder?" I walked away from her. "That's not our style."

She grabbed me and looked up at our building. "Lower your voice before somebody hears you."

I shook her off of me. "You tripping now. The last thing I'm gonna do is calm down. Do you even hear yourself talking? You being not rational."

BY SHAY HUNTER

"Think about it, if we beat her ass tomorrow what you think gonna happen? She's gonna snitch and we'll get locked up. All that's gonna do is give her more time to be with our boyfriends. I don't know about you but that won't work for me. Fuck that shit!"

"I get all of that, but murder, Barby? The fact that you can do this so easily makes me worried about myself around you. What you gonna do? Kill me too?"

She glared at me. "You know I wouldn't do anything to you. Not unless you don't follow the plan or fuck up mine."

I swallowed and scratched my arm because I didn't get the answer I wanted. "All I'm gonna say is that I'm not with this."

She rolled her eyes. "Before you say no just think about it. Think long and hard about what that kind of money split two ways would do for us. What it will do for our lives."

"Nah, you mean split three ways. Even if I said yes Paris's name on the policy too or have you forgotten?"

She scratched her head and her eyes bulged. "Yeah...I did forget." She walked away from me and then hurried back like she had the perfect answer for our problem. "Unless we take her out too. We gonna murder one person why not murder two?" She pointed at me and her eyes were wild.

"What's wrong with you?" I pushed her away. "You not thinking sanely now!"

She blinked a few times and sat on the step in front of the building. For some reason I followed her when I should've been running in the other direction.

"This is all I know, that we need to make Tabitha pay for all the sneaky shit she's done to us, Kaden. And that if we don't make it final she may come back on us in some way. Is that what you want? To be locked up while she's out in the world?"

"No…"

"So why not finish her once and for all and get the money too? It's a win-win situation for everybody."

"How do I know you didn't have this plan all along?"

Her eyes lowered and she looked like another person. "You don't, Kaden, but I'm asking you to trust me."

CHAPTER FIFTEEN
CHAVIV

*T*he moment Chaviv knocked on the door, Lexi jumped on him as he walked her into her apartment, slamming the door behind them. He was able to handle her tiny frame because she only weighed 95 pounds and that was mostly ass.

He smiled at her and said, "Now that's how you say hello to a nigga." He kissed her again while walking with her slowly. "What you up to? Hoping I'd stop by? If so your wish has been answered."

"Daddy, I didn't know you were coming," she said seductively kissing him all over his face. "I would've cooked you something. But I'm so glad you hit me and said you out front."

Her two long braids hung down her back and he grabbed both, pulled them back and kissed her neck like he was preparing to bite into her flesh. Eager to get inside of her, he carried her to the sofa, bent her over and tore her underwear off. Filled with lust, for a second he looked at her slim thick frame and licked his lips. He was deciding on if he would go to the front or back.

He removed his gun, sat it on the side of the couch and undid his jeans.

Lexi eyed the weapon and smiled.

"What you want tonight? The rough or soft?"

When she popped her ass cheeks he figured taking the buns would be as good a place as any to start. He couldn't help but marvel at how such a tiny body could take a long dick but that was her business not his. They didn't do a lot together but when it came to fucking they seemed to make music.

"Ummm, that feels so good, Chaviv. Why you got me shaking like this? Damn you know how to fuck me."

"You like this huh?" He continued, taking his time with her pussy, despite having places to go and people to see.

Chaviv continued to drive into her asshole like a construction worker drilling into concrete. It was always her favorite and he could tell she loved it by the way she bit her bottom lip. When she backed into him he grabbed her two braids and hammered into her until he exploded into her warm flesh. Her asshole got as juicy as her pussy which was another thing he loved about her.

Once done he picked her up, placed her on the sofa and flopped next to her. Out of breath, he didn't bother to pull up his pants, which sat at his ankles. But Lexi, in pleasing mode, pulled her panties up, dropped to her knees and slid his pants up. She left the buckle unfastened as well as his pants. "Thanks, sexy."

"Now that, that's out the way what brings you here?" She asked looking up at him. "Don't get me wrong, your dick is always welcome here." She slid her fingers along the middle of her stomach and into the entrance of her pussy hole. "But...still...something's up. So lets be real and talk about it."

He chuckled and shook his head. "Why is it that you know me? I never understood that about you."

"It's call giving a fuck." She shrugged. "Plus we been doing this for a long time and I can feel when something is off with you, Chaviv. You know that."

"But how?"

She giggled. "Well if I tell you all my secrets I'll have to kill you."

He glared at her. "Is that right?"

"What you think?" She giggled.

He nodded. "You know, you the only one I let talk to me like that." He paused. "Nah, for real, answer the question. How you know something sitting on my mind?"

"I don't know, Chaviv." She shrugged. "The fuck game be different. The conversation be shorter and your eyes be intense." She sat on his lap so that she could look into his eyes. "But last and most importantly, you don't come through here any day of the week unless it's Sunday."

He nodded and looked out into her living room at nothing in particular. "I think she may be cheating on me. Tabitha. And I don't know how to feel about that. I got shit to do in these streets, Lexi. Worrying about some bitch letting niggas dump off in her shouldn't be on my list of problems."

She squinted. "And yet it is."

He nodded. "Yeah, it is."

She giggled. "Well, I always said them bitches at that crib stay keeping up shit. As a matter of fact, now that I think about it...I do remember hearing something 'bout that." She pointed at him. "The cheating thing."

His eyes widened. "What you hear? And why you ain't tell me before now?"

"The last time I brought up your girlfriend you almost broke my jaw. So I don't bring up her name unless you wanna talk. Those the rules between us and I haven't changed them. You know that."

"Well what you hear?"

"I heard from somebody who knows Dandre that Tabitha and him have been fucking each other for as long as yah been together. On the low."

"Nah...you ain't here no shit like that." His nostrils flared. "I know you ain't here no shit like that because you know I would go mad in this bitch."

She shrugged. "Okay, if you say – "

He grabbed her shoulders and interrupted her sentence. "You ain't here no shit like that! Say it! I want to hear you say it out your lips!"

Her eyes widened. "You right...I didn't hear nothing like that." Her body trembled under his grasp. "Tabitha would never cheat on you. Whoever said that got it on bad info and I'm sorry I brought it to you, Chaviv."

He nodded and released her. She quickly rubbed her throbbing arms. "I thought so."

She looked down and frowned at him. "Chaviv, I've been waiting on you to dump Tabitha from the day I saw you at my friend's housewarming. And I knew if I ever had a chance to be with you I wouldn't fuck it up." She kissed him on the lips. "But you can't keep coming over her taking your anger out on me. If them niggas over there got you wrong, do something about it. But don't leave no witnesses when you do. Kill everybody standing. That's my only advice."

He shook his head and the psycho disposition he possessed reared its ugly head. "They playing me ain't they? All of 'em."

She nodded yes. "What's going on? What made you ask me?"

"Both of her roommates said she's fucking Dandre. Even the bitch he dealing with." He wiped his hand down his face in frustration. "This shit seems all over the place."

"Is she worth getting in your head?"

"Nah, but I'm not a sucka-ass-nigga, Lexi. I don't let people run games on me without answering to it. If I kill him, I'll kill her too." He looked into her eyes. "Believe that."

"Then don't be disrespected. Do what you gotta do?"

He frowned and then smiled. "Fuck all that." He waived the air. "You trying to go another 'round?"

"You said the magic words."

When Chaviv walked through Tabitha's apartment he was taken aback at how it smelled like a pizza kitchen. The girl definitely knew how to cook. He grabbed a slice of pizza off the kitchen counter and Tabitha smiled at him. "Well?" She said, wiping her long hair over her shoulder.

"Well what?" he sighed with a mouth full of food. He just got into some pussy and was in full guilt mode. "Don't start asking me where I been, Tab. I – "

She placed her hand on his chest to calm him down. "Bae, bae, I'm asking how you like the pizza. It's from scratch." She shook her head. "I swear I hate when you assume you know everything I'm 'bout to say. I'm not as heavy as you think."

Just as she said that Dandre came out of Barby's room. He nodded at Chavio and attempted to shake his hand but Chavio said, "Eating right now, bruh." He didn't fuck with him at all, especially after talking to Lexi.

Embarrassed, Dandre wiped his hand down his jeans. "Uh, no problem," he said, although he gave him the side eye. "Aye, Tab, you seen Barby? I wanted to talk to her about a few things."

"They went outside and I haven't – "

Suddenly Paris's bedroom door came flying open. "Somebody call 911! Something's wrong with Maceo again!"

CHAPTER SIXTEEN
PARIS

I can feel my eyes prickling with tears as I'm trying to compose myself. Trying to breathe and not pass out. Holding the phone against my ear I'm attempting not to allow this 911 dispatcher to make me angry. Why can't she see that I'm giving as much information as possible on Maceo's condition?

"Yes, ma'am, like I said blood is everywhere!" I looked at Maceo and he's convulsing so hard I think he's about to explode. "But you have to hurry because I don't think he will make it! Please send the ambulance now! Why yah waiting!"

Inside the room with me are Dandre, Tabitha, and Chaviv. They're trying to hold him down because several times he almost hit his head on the headboard but even they can't control him.

"Is he on drugs or was he using alcohol?" She said in a lazy manner, as if she didn't care.

"No, he hasn't been drinking or smoking anything! He was asleep and woke up convulsing!" I yelled at her. "Now get over here, bitch!"

I threw my cell phone across the room and tried my best to steady Maceo's body by calling his name but he doesn't hear me. When his eyes began to roll to the back of his head I feel faint and my legs feel like they've left my body.

"Maceo, you can't die on me," I said sobbing. "You can't die on me."

"He won't, Paris," Tabitha said softly. "Just keep praying and talking to him. He'll be fine, trust me."

I nodded and she pulled me into a strong hug which seemed to relax me. I needed to be away from Maceo and this entire ordeal because it was too much. All of this was too much. I knew this was related to me choking him and I was scared.

It took five minutes for the paramedics to get there and I was an emotional wreck when they arrived. My body ached and my temples felt as if they were throbbing. At first they thought they would have to take me too. But there was no way I was going to the hospital because I didn't want to be questioned on what caused the injury or have to witness him dying, a situation I was sure was to come.

Luckily for me Dandre went.

After telling the paramedics all I knew I sat on the edge of my bed and cried my eyes out. Tabitha walked up to Chaviv and said, "I'm gonna spend some time with her. I'll see you tomorrow okay?"

He nodded and kissed her on the lips before walking out.

When he was gone she closed my bedroom door and moved toward me slowly. "How you holding up, Paris?"

I wiped the tears with my knuckles. "I can't believe how he looked. Did you see his face?" I pointed at the closed door. "It wasn't him. That person wasn't my man! My perfect man!"

She exhaled. "Paris, it's not your—"

"Don't say that!" I pointed at her. "You don't know if it's my fault or not because you weren't with us. You don't know everything so don't lie to me."

She nodded. "Do you remember when I was telling you about my husband? Way before Chaviv was even thought of? It was a few months ago."

I looked at her and wiped more tears away. "Yeah, I think so…but I…I almost forgot you were married."

"Well we were together for three years, Paris." She looked out into my bedroom. "I was way too young to

BY SHAY HUNTER

be getting married but there was nothing else I wanted to do but be with him. I haven't been in love like that since then and I pray to God I never will again."

"Not even with Chaviv?"

"Girl, no," she waived the air. "Don't get me wrong, Chaviv is dope as fuck but I know he's a cheater and I'm okay with that. What I expect him to do is be fun for me when I need him." She shook her head. "Nah, this man was different. If he would've said kill myself and find my way back to him in spirit I would have done it without thinking."

My eyes widened. "Wow, you never told me that."

"It's not something I'm proud of but it's the truth." She dropped her hands in her lap and played with her fingertips. "But anyway we got into an argument one day. I caught him with a friend of mine and it tore me to pieces. She was a troublemaking bitch I was friends with who kept up shit. She had a man and everything. You never felt that kind of pain and I don't wish it on anybody I hate. It hurt that bad."

"Please say you killed him."

She giggled. "I did better than that, I left him and told him he could keep everything. I didn't answer my phone no matter how much he begged. And girl, he begged hard."

"What ended up happening?"

"He hung himself in my mother's bathroom. Can you believe that shit? He didn't do it in his house. He came over my mother's house just to hurt me. Told her I was expecting him and everything. All lies."

"Oh my gawd, Tabitha!" I covered my mouth with my fingers. "I know you were tore up."

"Girl, yes, it took three months of depression to realize it wasn't my fault. The mind will convince you of whatever you want if you talk to it enough. I even considered killing myself just to apologize to him for breaking his heart that badly. Thank God I didn't." She took a deep breath. "Now I know whatever you got going on is much different but if Maceo is sick it's not your fault, Tabitha."

I shook my head no because I knew the truth. We did something that we probably shouldn't have and he's been messed up ever since. The more I thought about it I started crying again. I cried because I didn't want him to die and I cried because I knew what was going to happen to Tabitha tomorrow in this apartment.

I needed an emotional release.

I walked over to my bedroom door and locked it. I needed to make sure that no one interrupted what I was about to say.

As I came back and sat down and talked to her I realized she was genuinely a nice person who was about to walk into something she wasn't prepared for with Kaden and Barby tomorrow. "Tabitha, you need to be careful."

She frowned. "Why you say that?"

"The girls don't trust you."

She stood up. "What you talking about?"

Suddenly there was a knock at my door. "Hey, Paris, is everything okay in there?" Barby asked. "I just watched Maceo be taken by the ambulance and I wanted to check on you. Why this door locked? Open it."

"Tab is here, uh, come back later."

"Oh…is Tabitha in there with you?"

For some reason I felt like she was testing me. Like she knew what I was about to tell Tabitha. About the plan to steal the rent money and to beat her up. Everything. "Yes, she's in here…"

There was a long moment of silence. "Hi, Tabitha."

"Hey, Barby, there's some extra pizza on the stove," Tab said to the door.

"Thank you."

Barby didn't walk away until thirty seconds later. I stood up and took Tabitha's hand and walked her over to the window so we could be as far away from the door as possible. "Listen, you aren't safe here, Tabitha."

"But why? I don't understand."

I took a deep breath. "Barby noticed that you've been spending a lot of time with Dandre."

"What?" she laughed. "You can't be serious. Please don't tell me that's why she's beefing with me lately. Acting all short and stuff."

I frowned. "Tab, this shit's serious."

"I'm not saying that it isn't. It's just that she has it all wrong about me and Dandre." She frowned. "Girl, no offense but he is definitely not my type. I could never do that to her."

Before she could finish telling me more there was another knock at the door. This time it was Kaden. "Aye, why yah in there being so secretive? Can we come in? We're worried about you too, Paris. Open the door."

I rolled my eyes. "Why? I'm talking to Tabitha right now. Come back in a little while."

"We just wanna know what happened with Maceo," Kaden continued. "Open the door." She started turning the knob but it was locked.

"He went to the hospital, Kaden."

"So you stayed with Tabitha instead of going with your man?" Barby said. "Seems kinda odd to me."

"I can take you to the hospital if you want," Kaden said. "I got my mother's car. She let me borrow it for a couple of days."

I sighed. They were really trying to get in here and it was spooking me out. "Kaden, just come back later. Please."

When she was gone I said, "This is serious, Tabitha. Did you see that shit?" I grabbed her hands. "Whether it's true or not, about you and Dandre, its what they believe," I whispered.

"Paris, Dandre is proposing to her." She said with a smile on her face. "I helped him pick out the ring. That's why we been sneaking around behind her back. The man is about to ask her to be his wife. He's not interested in me!"

I placed my hand on both sides of my face. I thought Tabitha was dirty too, even told Chaviv and now I felt beyond guilty. She was helping him give her a surprise. That's why you have to stay away from sneaky bitches like Barby. "No, Tabitha...you fucking with me."

"No...he's gonna ask. Probably at the party tomorrow."

"I knew something was wrong," I paused. "I knew that was not like you to be so dirty. I tried to tell them but nobody wanted to listen to me. Wait until she finds—"

KNOCK. KNOCK. KNOCK.

"WHAT?" I yelled to the door.

"HURRY UP AND COME OUT!" Barby yelled. "I WANNA TALK TO YOU!"

"I'M COMING NOW!" I grabbed Tabitha's hands. "Maybe you should tell her about the proposal. You see how desperate they are? They've become dangerous now. This whole thing has turned crazy."

Tabitha stood straight up, took a deep breath and smiled. With a confident aura she said, "Nope, the party is tomorrow. And I can't wait to see the look on her face when she realizes she was wrong about me. She was wrong about everything."

CHAPTER SEVENTEEN

BARBY

I was pacing in the living room with Kaden wondering what was going on in Paris's room. I knew Paris wasn't all in with our plan but now I had proof. There they were talking about us behind closed doors and leaving us out. If Paris thought I was gonna let it go like this she doesn't know me at all.

I smelled a traitor.

"Wow, can you believe this shit?" I whispered to Kaden. "Like they still in there even though we trying to come in." I pointed at the door. "Now you see why I say fuck Paris. She can get the bullet too. Lets kill both of them."

She shook her head. "And the bitch still didn't finish my hair." She ran her fingers through the small patch. "I mean look at it."

"I'll get one of my cousins to finish your hair before the party, don't worry 'bout that." I waved the air because she was talking about stupid shit. "We need to be thinking about what we gonna do tomorrow."

She frowned at me. "Both of them braid too hard." She ran her fingers through the unbraided section, still thinking about other nonsense. "I rather do it myself then to let them in my hair."

I rolled my eyes. "Well do it then!" I paused. "But what we gonna do about this matter?" I pointed at the door. "And what we gonna do about both of them?"

"Let's hear what she says first. I'm talking about Paris."

"We can't get in the—"

When the door opened Tabitha smiled at us. "Did yah get some pizza? I made it from scratch and Chaviv said it tasted really good. I hope he didn't take it all with him."

"Nah, we gonna get some though," I said. "It's still on the stove."

"Cool," she said.

From Paris' opened door I could see her sitting on the bed with her back faced us. "Is everything okay in there?" I asked Tabitha even though I was looking into Paris' room from the living room. "She seems like she's taking things really bad."

"Yeah, Maceo had a seizure so we waiting to see what's gonna happen at the hospital. Paris just called his family." She sighed. "He was really bad, the worst I've ever seen him. They don't even know if he'll make it."

"Aw," I said, realizing I probably sounded fake. "Well let me go talk to her then because she's probably really sad."

"Okay, I'm gonna prep the rest of the food for tomorrow. She walked to the kitchen.

When Kaden tried to follow me to Paris's room I turned around and extended my hand to stop her in her toe steps. "Nah, let me go by myself," I whispered. "I want to try and feel her out first."

Her eyes widened. "Why? I wanna know too."

"Girl, just wait," I said a little louder. "I'll call for you."

I walked into Paris' room and closed the door in her face before she could say anything else. Carefully I eased around until I was standing in front of her. "Paris, you good in here?"

She shrugged. "Are you okay in here?" She said with an attitude. "Really? That's all the fuck you have to say to me?"

I frowned. "Why you say that?"

"Yah banging at the door like you crazy or I stole something from you. And now when you in here the only thing you can ask is if I'm okay? I thought you were gonna tell me there was a fire or something, Barby. But the fake shit. You starting to get on my nerves with all of this."

I dropped my hands down by my sides. Glaring at her I said, "Did you tell her anything?"

"Nah...I told you I wasn't gonna say anything about you beating her up. It's stupid though."

I put my hands on my hips. "Oh really?"

"You are so wrong about Tabitha." She smiled like she was going crazy. "I know you mad at her for whatever reasons but trust me when I say you're completely off and you need to get another place if you gonna do it but leave that girl alone."

"So now yah best friends?"

"No but I—"

"What she do, suck your tits or something when the door was closed? If you ask me you were in here long enough."

She giggled but I could tell it was an angry laugh. "Now you being real dumb."

"Did you tell her something or not?"

"I said nah!"

I didn't believe her. "So what yah in her with the door closed for? You making me think you not loyal to—"

She jumped up. "BITCH, MY BOYFRIEND WAS JUST TAKEN AWAY IN AN AMBULANCE AND YOU COMING IN HERE LIKE THAT? ARE YOU THAT FUCKING SELFISH? YOU HAVE TO BE!"

I stepped away from her. "I was just—"

"Just what, Barby? Only caring about what you got going on in your life?" She paused. "That's your problem, you too fucking conniving! You think the world owes you something and me included!"

I moved away some more until I couldn't move any further and my back was against the wall. "I'm not selfish, I was just asking because—"

"Maceo may die and for real I don't have time for any of this." She started to cry but I think it was to throw me off her trail so I had no pity for the chick. She was definitely holding something back. "Is that what you want? For my man to die? Will you feel better about putting all this on my shoulders then?"

"Paris, how you sound?" I paused. "I fuck with Maceo. You know that. Why would I want him hurt?"

She flopped on the bed and I walked up to her slowly, before sitting next to her. "What's really going on?"

She ran her hand down her face. "I think I fucked up."

"Is this what you were talking to Tabitha 'bout?"

"Kinda. But I didn't want to tell her everything."

I inched closer. "So what happened?" I rubbed her back like I saw Tabitha do so many times. It felt ridiculous. I don't even know why she did it. "To Maceo?"

"You can't tell anybody."

"Paris! As much shit as—"

"I'm serious. I'm about to share with you something I never told anybody because I have to get it off my chest or I'm gonna explode. I can't hold on to this secret anymore."

"Okay, so what happened?"

"Maceo comes over after getting off the plane the other day and he wanted me to...he wanted me to do something we always do."

"Well? What was it?"

"He wanted me to choke him with this tie, while he was jerking off. So he could cum and lose his breath at the same time. I did it and I think I held it too long around his throat and now he's messed up."

"You can't be serious."

She frowned. "See, this is why I didn't wanna tell anybody."

"I'm not judging you. I'm just asking if you serious."

"This would be the last thing I would joke about, Barby. That's on everything."

"So what you think happen to him?" I tried to sound concerned but I wanted to get to the part about Tabitha and the ass beating she had coming tomorrow. "After you finished that night?"

She shrugged. "Maybe since oxygen got cut off so long from his brain he ain't been the same. I'm just guessing because I really don't know, Barby. I have to wait for the hospital to call. I just knew I couldn't stand to see him like that."

"Wow, I had no idea," I said. The whole time I'm thinking this bitch is crazy. Who has sex with choking? "I feel so bad for you. I'm sorry."

"How could you know? It's not something I tell anybody and...you know what...I need some air now because I'm not sure if I should've even told you.

Maceo would kill me if he ever found out." She got up, opened the door and walked out.

I watched her and smiled sinisterly.

Kaden trudged in with her half braided ass and we both stared at her leaving the apartment. "What the fuck was that?" Kaden whispered. "Her face is bloodshot red. What you do? Punch her or something?"

"I don't trust her," I said, still looking at the door although she was gone.

"Why you say that?"

"She told me something that fucked up my mind but I think she did it because she doesn't want me to know what her and Tabitha were really talking about." I looked at her. "We gonna have to watch her. Closely."

CHAPTER EIGHTEEN
BARBY

"Ma, I know you think this is like the last time I got into an argument with my roommate but it's different." I was lying face up on my bed talking to my mother on the phone. "This girl is way worse than anybody I—"

"Where did I go wrong with you, Barby? I pray to God nightly for an answer and I haven't gotten one yet. So I'm asking you. Where did I go wrong? What didn't I do that you needed? Tell me now so I can pray on it."

"Ma, what you talking about?"

"Why you so bitter? Why you believe the world owes you something? Huh? Why don't you do your best to make sure you a nice person? That way you can witness others treating you nicely in return? You have to be miserable."

I rolled my eyes. "You think I'm a monster."

"No, what I think is that every girl who has come into your life, after awhile does something wrong to you. To hear you tell it. Where's your part in all of this? What do you do wrong?"

My throat bobbed a little as I suppressed a cry. "So you saying I'm lying? I'm making all this up? That Tabitha is out to take Dandre from me?"

"What? No! Where did you hear that from?"

"That's how it sounds, mama."

"What I'm saying is that you're a troublemaker, girl. It's as plain as the lips on your face. You done been in this girl's house for a year. She cooks for you and the others, makes a home and you hating. What for, Barby? I gave you the name Barby so you can play well with others, like the doll. But you are an animal!"

"Mama!" I whimpered.

"Whatever you're doing or about to do I'm begging you to go the other way. You have Dandre don't you? Build a life with him and be happy. Leave that girl alone. Don't—"

I hung up on my mother.

I don't know why I expected her to take my side. She's the same hater of me she's always been and that won't stop no time soon. When my door opened Dandre walked inside. "What you doing, sexy? I called your name to come into the living room but you ain't answer me."

"I was talking to my mother."

"She still mad at you?"

I laughed but for real it wasn't funny. I sat up and when he sat on the bed I straddled him so that we were looking at each other. "How is Maceo? I heard you went to the hospital."

"Bad." He exhaled and rubbed my ass. "He might not make it."

My eyes widened. "You serious? I thought he was gonna be aight."

He shook his head. "I never seen him like that. When you look in his eyes he looks like he not there. Like I'm looking at the wall. It's crazy as fuck. I needed to smoke a J when I left him my mind was so messed up."

My eyes widened. For a second I thought about what my mother said, about me being a troublemaker but she don't know shit about me. She ain't nothing to me.

Tabitha is the real monster in this house.

I'm like a journalist. All I do is report the news.

"I know what happened." I said kissing him. "I know why Maceo in the hospital fighting for his life." He kissed me again but his eyes remained opened. I separated our lips. "Why you looking at me like that?"

"What happened? Why you stop? I thought he had a seizure or something. Right?"

I looked down and back at him. "Well that's part of it but not the whole story."

"What's the other part?"

"Paris did something to him," I grinned. "And if he dies she gonna wish she jumped off a building when the police find out." I giggled after hearing myself talk.

He rose up, placed me on my feet and walked away from me. Leaning against the wall he said, "What you saying, bae? I don't like police talk when I'm in the room. So what you mean by all of this?"

"I'm not calling the police. I was just—"

"Stop fucking around. What you saying? What happened to Maceo?"

"I don't know a lot but Paris told me they into some real freaky shit. I mean some real freaky shit where they be choking each other out. Next thing she knew—"

He looked down at the floor. "Why you doing this?"

My eyebrows rose. "Doing what?"

"Why would you tell anybody what you just said to me? Even if it was true? Don't you know if that got out that girl could get locked up for life? Huh? Why you don't use your brain?"

"But—"

"You gotta stop being selfish, Barby. You too fine for that shit. You gotta learn to stop being petty or you gonna wake up and nobody gonna fuck with you. That's exactly how it happens. It starts with the snitching type shit and then you an outcast."

"I—"

"I finally understand why these broads in DC don't fuck with you." He pointed at me. "Stay outta dumb shit or you gonna lose a real nigga." He walked out the door and left it open.

Five seconds later with me standing in the middle of the floor Kaden walked inside. She was getting on my nerves. Every time I wanted a chance to process everything that happened to me or that I hear, here she comes. "What was that about?"

"Paris turned on me. And she had Dandre turn on me too."

"What? I thought it was Tabitha?"

"It's both them bitches. But I'm mainly talking about Paris now."

She scratched the unbraided portion of her scalp. "Wait, you confusing me, Barby. Who we beefing with? Because now it sounds like everybody."

I grabbed my cell phone on the bed. "Dandre said Paris is a snake. I'm telling you what he told me a second ago. He said she was talking behind our back. Said Maceo told him on the way to the hospital not to trust me. You can believe me or not, I don't care." I knew I was lying but it was the only way people believed me.

"Wait..." she put her hands out, palms in my direction. "Exactly what did he say?"

"Does it matter?" I grabbed her hand and walked into the bathroom in my room. "Come with me right quick. I'm gonna fix everybody who wronged me."

I closed the door and sat on the toilet. "What we doing in here?" She frowned. "You got me all kinds of confused."

I dialed a number and placed it on speakerphone. "911 emergency may I have your location?"

"It's 1234 Murdock St, Washington DC."

"How can I help you?" the operator asked.

"Yes, a Maceo Carter was taken out of my house today and I have some information on what happened to him. Some information that may be useful in case he dies."

"Ma'am, was he attacked?"

"Yes, he was choked by Paris Porter and yah betta come get This murderer off the streets." I hung up and smiled at Kaden. "Now I got that bitch."

Her jaw dropped. "Wait, did you just call the police?"

"Yep." I grinned. "I'm tired of fucking with these chicks 'round here. They better recognize who I am."

She shook her head. "I can't believe you did that."

I rolled my eyes. "Stop tripping and get over it."

"What if he dies?" She moved closer. "Paris going away for life, Barby. I wish you hadn't done that. Why did you do that?"

"So what if she goes to prison." I shrugged. "Maybe she deserves that shit, I don't know and what do I care."

KNOCK. KNOCK. KNOCK.

"You gonna pay for that, Barby," Kaden whispered while pointing at me. "That was a bad move. A very bad move."

"Aye, Kaden, you in there?" Lakota out here in the living room to see you," Tabitha said on the other end of the door.

"Oh my God!" Kaden said covering her mouth. "Dandre and Lakota in the house together," she whispered. "They haven't seen each other since Lakota stabbed him." She faced the door. "I'm coming now, Tabitha!" She yelled. "Tell him to go in my room and wait for me."

"Okay…" Tabitha said before walking away.

"Oh so what, you don't want the money we talked about now?" I asked grabbing Kaden's wrist before she left. "Because ain't no turning back on the plan. I called in for reinforcements in case you try to back out."

"What does that supposed to mean? Reinforcements."

"Don't fuck with me, Kaden." I said glaring at her.

"You know what, none of this shit was about Dandre was it? You just a jealous bitch who loves hating on other females. And you gonna get yours."

"And you gonna get it right with me, kitty cat."

She shook her head and walked out, slamming the door behind herself.

CHAPTER NINETEEN
KADEN

He acted like we hadn't fucked in years as he had me pressed against the floor, my legs around his waist as his mouth covered mine while I sucked his tongue. He was breathing so hard it sounded like he was running a marathon and hearing how much he wanted me had me juicing up so much our bodies slid on one another with sweat.

"Keep it like that, Lakota. You haven't fucked me this good in a long time and that dick just right tonight." I told him as he continued to stroke my inner walls. "I love you so much and I'll do anything for you. You know that right?"

He softly bit my chin as he spread my cheeks wider apart as if he was trying to rip me in two. "You *better* do anything for me. You better kill for me too." He moaned louder. "Fuck, Kaden, your pussy stay tight, just the way I love it, girl. Don't let nobody touch my shit! Because I'd kill your fucking ass. I don't care what we do you gonna always belong to me. You better know that shit."

"Never anybody else, baby." I moaned as I continued to buck my hips and push into him. "This right here is all yours. Ain't nobody fucking with you."

"I know it is sexy, bitch." He sucked my bottom lip. "With your fine ass."

"So I don't look like a nigga now do I?" I said fucking him harder.

"Can't no nigga make me feel like this. You talking crazy."

The dirtier he talked the closer I came to exploding on his balls. The way he fucked me it was like he was trying to prove he wanted me back. And I appreciated it because just thinking about losing him had me wanting to jump out a window. So I swerved my hips as much as possible and could tell he was on the verge of busting inside of me.

"I'm 'bout to cum, Kaden. Keep working like that, bae. I'm almost there."

I didn't respond because I came a few seconds ago and was waiting on him to get his. To help him out I turned over and raised my ass in the air so he could see inside of me. I could feel his dick pulsating and when he was satisfied he collapsed on top of my back.

With hot breath on my neck he said, "She put me out, Kaden. That stupid bitch put me out." His comment was out of nowhere and it was like we didn't have sex.

I got up, snatched some tissue from the dispenser and wiped my pussy before giving him some clean tissue. "Who...who putting you out?" I tossed it in the trash.

"My girl."

That stung.

I flopped next to him on the bed. "So, what you gonna do now? Where you gonna live?"

"I don't know, Kaden. I spoke to my cousin in Atlanta and he told me I could come stay by him." He shrugged and looked me in the eyes. "I may have to do that. I don't want to be that far from you but I might not have a choice." He paused. "For now I'm confused."

"Atlanta, Lakota? I can't have you going that far."

"You think I want to do that shit?" He crawled on the bed and lie face up with one hand behind his head the other on his belly. Dick resting back in it's shell. "But ain't nothing for me out here."

"What about me?"

THE ONE YOU SHOULDN'T TRUST   173

"That won't keep me safe."

"But what made her put you out, Lakota?"

"I don't know but I think Dandre had something to do with it. My girl friends with Dandre's cousin. I think he told her to put me out but I can't be sure."

"Are you gonna at least try to get something out here? In DC? Or Maryland? Maybe even Virginia? Before you leave everything you've known?"

"No...I mean...Dandre may be still tripping." He paused. "I feel like he's gonna strike at any time."

He reached in his jeans on the bed, pulled out a pack of cigarettes and lit one. I hated tasting cigarettes on his lips but got used to it with time. "I don't want you to leave, Lakota."

"It's easier said than done.

"So if I come up with a plan, for us to have some money and a place here will you stay?" I exhaled, hoping he'd say yes.

"What you talking 'bout?"

I moved closer to him. "I may have a plan for some money. But Lakota, I can't have you leaving me. If we gonna be together you gotta fully commit or else it ain't gonna work between us. My plan means somebody may get hurt."

"I'm committing, baby."

He didn't even ask who, all he cared about was the money. "So how I know you won't change your mind later? After I get the money? How I know you won't make fun of how I look again? Or make another girl your number one?"

"Because I'm here, Kaden. I wouldn't be here if I wasn't feeling you. You know that."

I stared into his eyes for as long as I could until mine dried out. Afterwards I blinked a few times and took a deep breath. "Okay, so you can stay here for tonight and tomorrow. After that we gonna get a hotel or something. Just give me a few weeks and I promise we gonna be fine. I'm gonna get us some money."

BARBY

I called Dandre several times and he didn't answer the phone. He must've still been mad at me.

Hungry, I went to the kitchen and Tabitha was in there as usual, cleaning up like a waitress who knew everybody's business. She was wiping the counter when she turned around and saw me. "Oh, hey, I saw Dandre storm out right before Lakota got here. I'm glad too. Everything okay with Dandre? They not still beefing are they? Because we can't have that stabbing stuff anymore."

I smiled at this bitch. "Why, Tab?"

"Why what?"

"Why you so concerned what me and Dandre do?"

Her eyebrows rose. "Barby, I have to talk to you about something. I was gonna wait but I can tell by the look in your eyes that you have it all wrong about me."

I crossed my arms over my chest. "What the fuck you wanna tell me?"

"I know you think something is up with me and Dandre but you have it all wrong. I'm not interested in him and never have been."

"Do I know that, Tabitha?" I asked rolling my eyes. "Do I have it fucking—"

"He's proposing to you, Barby." She moved closer. "He's gonna ask you to be his wife at the party."

I covered my mouth and my entire body felt like it was overheating. My head felt light and it was as if I wasn't standing on my feet. "Don't play, Tabitha." I touched my chest. "Don't play like this because it would kill me."

"I wouldn't do that to you," she smiled. "And I feel bad that I told you because he asked me to help pick out the ring and everything. But I figured it was best you know than have those thoughts about me. Those bad thoughts."

"But...I..."

She stepped closer and grabbed one of my hands. "I would never fuck with your man or any of my friends' men. Why would you even think that way?"

"I...I'm..." I backed away from her and into the refrigerator. I'm about to kill this girl for nothing? "I didn't know. I thought...I thought the worst things about you. I...I thought you...you couldn't be trusted."

"Let it go...but whatever you do, please don't tell Dandre," she whispered. "I don't want him mad at me for ruining his surprise. Let him come to you and ask you to be his wife. Let him think you don't know." She hugged me and walked out and into her room.

I stood in the middle of the kitchen feeling dumb when Kaden walked up to me. "I want in, Barby!" She paced the floor and I realized that once again when I wanted to collect my thoughts she appeared. I could smell the sex and cigarette smoke on her.

"Are you listening, Barby?" Kaden repeated stepping up to me. I stared at that unbraided portion on top of her head and started to cut it. It got on my nerves as well as everything else.

"What do you want in on?"

"I want in on the cash thing with Tab." She looked behind her and back at me. "Let's get that insurance money. Together."

I couldn't talk. My mouth opened but nothing came out.

"Barby, we still down right?"

Silence.

"Barby, we still down right?"

"Yes...yeah...of course."

CHAPTER TWENTY
PARIS

I finally went to the hospital and had just gotten home when Barby approached me at the door. What was wrong with this girl? It was the day of the party and my mind was doing flips after just seeing Maceo in a catatonic state.

He was officially deemed brain dead and his family was trying to make a decision if they should authorize the hospital to pull the plug. So the last thing I felt like doing was talking to Barby. But that didn't stop her from walking up to me and invading my space.

"How are you?" She whispered following me through the living room. "Can I do anything?"

I trudged into my room and she was on my heels. "Not good, Barby." I flopped down. "But what can I do?"

"So what they saying?" She sat on the bed and I leaned against the wall not trying to be close to her. "About Maceo? He gonna make it?"

"He's brain dead, Barby. So no, it doesn't look like he's gonna make it."

She covered her mouth with her fingertips and she looked super fake. I can't deal with this girl right now. "Oh my gawd, you lying!"

"No, Barby," I rolled my eyes. "I'm not lying."

"Can I do anything for you?" She scooted closer to me. "Maybe get you some breakfast? I'm no Tabitha but I can wrestle up something if you want. The refrigerator packed with the food for tonight so I'll have to make it work but—"

"Leave her alone tonight, Barby," I said seriously. "That's what you can do for me."

She blinked several times and looked around. For some reason in that moment I realized I was dealing with a mad woman. "What you mean leave her alone?" She played with one of her red locs.

I leaned in closer. "Don't do whatever you're planning to do to Tabitha."

She rolled her eyes. "You still protecting that chick after all this time?"

When I looked at her she didn't look as angry as she did before. I wasn't sure but I had a feeling she knew all of her opinions were wrong about Tabitha. In the past whenever I had anything to say about Tabitha that contradicted what she felt her nostrils would flare and she would tense up.

But now I think she knows.

Maybe she'll leave her alone after all.

Or maybe she's so crazy that she doesn't care.

"I'm protecting her because what you think went down is not what went down," I continued. "Leave her alone. I'm begging you."

"You love her so much don't you?"

"I care about her."

She frowned. "Everybody loves Tabitha." She took a deep breath and let it out slowly. "But sadly, your world is about to rock. Or, collapse."

My eyes widened. "What you mean?"

"You have something coming your way and its all her fault. Tabitha is not the person you think she is and I was right about her all along." She pointed at me. "Soon everyone will see."

I moved closer. "Can you say whatever you gotta say and stop beating around the bush?"

"I'm not sure but I think I heard her call the cops on you." She giggled. "Last night."

I held my stomach. "Fuck you talking about?"

"Like I said I'm not sure but the police got called."

"She called the police about what? I didn't do anything."

She shrugged. "Again, I'm not sure but I walked by her room and I could've sworn I heard her telling the cops about you and Maceo. And the choking thing."

"But I didn't tell anybody but you about Maceo!" I stood up and walked in front of her. "Please say you didn't do that, Barby. Please say you aren't that evil!"

"Like I said I heard Tabitha —"

I smacked her and for the first time she seemed genuinely scared. I hit her again just because. I was about to claw out her eyes when there was banging at the front door.

KNOCK. KNOCK. KNOCK.

I climbed off her body, left my room and headed to answer it. The moment I opened it three police officers rushed inside. One of them, a big man with an angry face flashed his large silver badge. "Are you Paris Porter?"

"Uh….I…"

"ARE YOU PARIS PORTER?" He yelled.

"Yes…I…yes…" My words flitted around in my mouth.

"You're under arrest for the murder of Maceo Carter."

I couldn't believe this was happening. I was whisked around and handcuffs were slapped on my wrists. "But I didn't do anything. Why are you taking me away?"

"Well if you're innocent that will be discussed in court," the officer said. "Now it's time to go."

Tears rolled down my eyes and when I looked across the living room I saw Barby staring at me with a sly smile on her face. When our eyes made contact she tried to appear sad but it was obvious what happened.

This wasn't Tabitha's fault.

This was all her doing.

Everything evil that happened here was her doing.

I don't know how but I needed to get in contact with Tabitha like yesterday. This chick was selfish and dangerous and Tabitha had to leave this apartment if she wanted to be safe.

BARBY

Paris did just what I thought she would do. Make two phone calls here to try and get in touch with Tabitha while in jail. But because I'm as smart as I am I made sure that I blocked all jail calls. So Kaden's cousin from down south would be short too.

Oh well.

All I knew was this, Paris wasn't about to fuck up my shit.

I don't care what she thought.

When Tabitha walked in the apartment with Kaden holding more food bags I approached them. "I got bad news, guys." I tried to put on my best performance ever. I tried to act like I really, really cared about people and things when I didn't. "It's about Paris."

They both walked over and placed the bags on the table. Tabitha placed her hands on her hips. "What...what is it?" She looked me up and down, as if trying to see if I was hurt. "What happened? Say something."

"First off Maceo died." I could've said that nicer but like I said I didn't care.

Kaden looked like she was gut punched. "No! Please don't say that."

"It was confirmed earlier so it's not a joke." I said. "His parents just called to say he didn't make it. They were very distraught but wanted us to know so they called."

"Did anything else happen, Barby?" Tabitha continued, her body trembling. "Because you look...you look like something else is on your mind." She touched her forehead.

"The cops arrested Paris about an hour ago." I sighed. "They took her into custody. I tried to help but they pushed me away and told me to stay out of it. There was nothing I could do."

I saw tears immediately fill the wells of Kaden's eyes. "Oh, no! But why? This isn't her fault. She didn't do anything but try to take care of him! Why would they do that?"

"Exactly!" Tabitha said.

"Actually, Tabitha, it kinda is her fault." I smiled. "You don't know everything because Paris was trying to keep it on the low. But Maceo's blood is on her hands."

"What?" She paused. "Why you say that?"

"Actually there's a lot about her and Maceo you didn't know. I never told you because I wanted to keep you out of it but those two were really freaky. Into some sadistic shit. The type of shit you go to hell for."

"What does that have to do with Maceo?" Tabitha asked.

"Because she —"

"Wow, you way out of line, Barby," Kaden said walking away. "You're fucking gross and out of line!" She slammed her bedroom door.

CHAPTER TWENTY-ONE

KADEN

I was on the phone, sitting on my bed talking to Lakota, doing my best not to cry out loud. She called the police on that girl and she got arrested. The worst part is I tied myself into Barby's world and I didn't see an escape.

Now I was a prisoner too. I needed the money and I needed to be away from Barby.

The door was locked but I was still worried she would come in and kill me, even though I knew she couldn't get inside. "She didn't care, Lakota," I whispered, looking at the door as if she would bust in, in any moment. "Like, she called the cops and Paris got arrested and she didn't care. What kind of person is she?"

"Wow, I ain't know your people got down like that."

"Me either. So what can I do?"

"You don't do nothing, Kaden," he said firmly. "What you mean what you do?" He chuckled. "If you get involved you'll be no better than her. A snitch. Stay out of it, K."

"So I'm 'spose to let her sit in jail and rot?" I paused. "Lakota, this seems so wrong." I tossed myself face up on my bed. "I feel so bad for her."

"Did she do it or not?"

I stood up. "I don't know but—"

"See, you don't even have the facts and it's none of your business, bae. If she ain't 'spose to be in there she won't be long. Let stuff play out on it's own. Without your help for once! Besides, you got other things to worry about like me. I can't move on the streets and I need a crib and some money. What's up with that plan? Or is Paris all you worried about these days? Don't neglect me, baby girl."

"You're right." I turned on my side and scratched my scalp. "I'm just...fucked up by it all." I sighed. "But don't worry. I'm gonna get some money for sure."

"I hope so. Because right now I'm homeless and—"

KNOCK. KNOCK.

I turned around and Barby came inside without my permission. She was holding a key to my door. Where did she get it from? "You still on the phone? Because I really need to talk to you about some things."

I smiled and it dropped away. I smiled and it dropped away again. I felt like a robot or a broken doll. She was so scary. "Yeah, I'm still talking to—"

"Go 'head and kick it with her," Lakota said. "I'll rap to you later 'bout everything else."

I sat the phone down and she walked deeper into my room, closing the door behind herself. "How did you get in? I locked my door."

"Oh, girl don't worry about that. I had keys made awhile ago, after you locked yourself out that time remember?"

I didn't.

"So you mad at me now?" She continued. "Just like the world it's my fault once again."

"You called the cops," I whispered. "And now—"

"Are you still with it or not?" She seemed short. "I don't have time for all this other stuff."

My eyebrows rose. "What you talking about all this other stuff?"

"I'm talking about the plan for Tabitha tonight. Because whether you in or not I'm pushing forward, Kaden. I want that money and it's mine. Do you hear me? It belongs to me!"

I rubbed my throbbing temples. "What happens if I say no? You gonna call the cops on me too?"

"How you sound?"

"You can't be trusted, Barby." I threw my arms up and they fell back down at my sides. "You can't be trusted because your emotions rule you. If you have that attitude how I know when shit goes down that you won't turn on me?"

"So I'm a snitch?"

"Yes!"

She looked at the door and back at me. "Maybe I am." She shrugged. "Who cares? And keep your voice down."

"How do I know, Barby? I'm waiting for an answer."

"Because you got to trust me."

I laughed. "Yeah aight."

"Okay I'll be honest. Yeah I may have gone a little too far with Paris but guess what, the damage is done isn't it?" She paused. "And even if she didn't get locked up it never meant our plan was not going down."

I scratched my head. "So what *is* this plan?"

"Well first off I called in for a little help. Like I told you last night."

My jaw opened. "So you were serious? You getting more people involved?"

"We need them."

"For what, Barby?"

"The body. How we gonna get it out without muscle?"

I felt like I wanted to throw up. Instead of answering I walked toward the door and she stopped me by grabbing my arm like I was a little girl getting into trouble. "You gotta decide tonight. You either with me or you against me. And trust me, you don't want to be against me."

"You a fucking monster."

She giggled. "You know what, I'm starting to think I am. And I like it."

TABITHA

I was on the phone in my room trying to get a hold of Paris in Jail but it wasn't working. Everyone was unhelpful. "Yes, ma'am, I've been trying to get more information on her but—"

"She hasn't been booked yet," the officer on the phone said. "Apparently she's in holding."

I frowned because they weren't giving me enough information. "So what that mean? I need to know what to do."

"It means we have 24 hours to get her into the system. And it also means you'll have to wait."

I paced the floor. "Listen, listen, I don't know what someone said but whatever they claimed she did she didn't do. And I need her home. You hear me? I *need* her home!"

"What you mean you need her home?"

I remained still and took a deep breath. Desperation was probably all in my voice. "She just needs to be home is all I'm saying."

"And like I said you have to call back, young lady."

When I looked at my screen and saw the call was ended I looked at Chaviv who was lying in my bed, the sheet over the lower part of his body since we had sex. "I can't believe we just fucked and the first thing you do is jump up and call the police about a woman."

I sat the phone down, got on the bed and straddled him. "I'm worried about her."

He smiled and combed my hair with his fingers, so that it fell over my breasts. "I bet you are." He smiled. "You beautiful. You know that?" He paused. "But you also naive."

"Naive?" I pointed at myself. "What does that even mean?"

"Have you ever thought that maybe they aren't into you like you're into them? Even Paris?" He squeezed my nipple and it hurt a little. "Have you ever thought you playing yourself with the females in here? You're too nice, baby girl."

I pushed his fingers away. "Why you say that?"

"I'm just trying to see where your mind is." He paused. "You do all you can to make everyone feel comfortable but you put no time in figuring out if they deserve it or not."

I tried to get off of him and he grabbed my waist and positioned me back over his crotch. His limp dick next to my pussy. "None of these bitches in here fuck with you, Tab. Not a one of 'em. And they all gonna get what's coming to them in one way or another."

"You just saying that because —"

"I'm your nigga." He grabbed my face and pulled my head down so our eyes were looking into each other. "And I wouldn't lie to you." He let me go. "Now I'm sorry she got locked up because caging anybody is fucked up on the mental." He pointed at his head. "But you gotta let her deal with that on her own."

"Maybe you right."

"And don't feel bad about that, Tabitha," he said. "It's just how shit is. It's how the world is out there. I'm trying to protect you."

"I know...so what am I gonna do now? Put in an ad for another roommate?"

"I say we get a place of our own. Let's leave these chicks to it."

I laughed. Hard. "Chaviv, ain't nobody moving in with yo ass, nigga." I got off of him and grabbed my robe. "Now get up and clean your dick. It's time to start the day." I walked out the door.

CHAPTER TWENTY-TWO
DANDRE

*T*he trap music was on blast so loud they could hardly hear each other but each seemed to understand what was happening. Dandre stood in front of his best friends Keith and Mo-Mo, in Keith's garage thinking about his next moves. They were drinking beer and talking about their plans for the night, which included retaliation for Lakota stabbing him.

"So you actually think this nigga will be there?" Keith asked. "Even after what he did to your hand? You said it yourself he been dodging, and when you be at your folks' house he be missing in action."

Dandre pulled on the Jay in his hand. "Nigga, I'm positive he'll be there. He not expecting shit. He really thinking I'm green enough to let this go. Having his bitch talk to me and clown shit like that. Nah, he gonna be there."

Mo-Mo shook his head. "He worse than green because I wouldn't come within three feet of you after what he did." He shook his head and accepted the Jay from Dandre. "If we gonna move it gotta be tonight. But what about your folks? I know you don't want them getting hit if shit kicks off."

"I'll worry about that tonight," Dandre said before he nodded. "It won't be a problem."

"I gotta know this, man, why you wait a few days to push off?" Keith asked tossing an empty beer can into the metal trash, making a loud clinking noise. "This should've been done days ago."

"Because I wanted him to put his guards down," Dandre said. "And he's done that."

Keith nodded. "Truth is it doesn't matter if the nigga expecting the return or not." He said sinisterly. "He got it coming and he gonna have it tonight."

They all nodded, as weed smoke filled the room.

BARBY

I walked up to Dandre and looked into his eyes to let him know I was serious even though I'm lying my face off. "Listen, I know you think it was me but I want you to know it wasn't. I was as confused as everybody else when she got arrested. It wasn't—"

He laughed like I was a joke or a clown. Like somebody he had no love for. "Look, you need to be

196 BY SHAY HUNTER

out there helping your folks get ready for your little thing tonight."

"And I'm gonna help after I talk to you." I held his hands. "But I don't want you mad at me, Dandre. I want to prove to you that I can be a good — "

He frowned and tilted his head. "Be a good what? Snitch?"

I was so caught up with not wanting him to think I was the one who called the cops on Paris that I was about to let go that I knew about the proposal. I was going to say be a good wife. "Nothing, Dandre."

"Don't nothing, me, bitch." He paused. "What were you 'bout to say?"

"Nothing." My heart thumped.

He grabbed me by my shoulders and shook me. "For once stop fucking around and tell the truth. Fuck wrong with you lately? You not on the one like I thought."

I looked away and sighed. It was time to bust Tabitha's world. "Earlier today I was getting out the shower and I caught Tabitha frowning at me. She didn't know I was watching her but on the side of her eye she was looking at me like I did something wrong. Like she was jealous of me or something."

"And?"

"And she came out of nowhere and said she didn't understand what you wanted with me. And that she didn't understand how you wanted to marry me."

He scratched his scalp. "How come that don't sound like her?"

"Because she's good at making people think she's a nice person, Dandre! She good at this shit and everybody around me thinks differently. They think I'm the bad guy! Meanwhile she's ruining everybody's life. And my relationship with you."

He scratched his scalp and let his hand fall heavy downward. "So you telling me that she told you I was gonna...gonna make you my wife? And that she was jealous cuz of that?"

I nodded. "Yes and I'm so sorry, Dandre because I know you wanted it to be a surprise. But my answer is yes!"

He rushed past me and bolted out the door. Tabitha was in the kitchen and he grabbed her by the lower arm and took her outside.

When she was gone Kaden came up to me. "What was that about? He looked like he was about to fight forty men."

198 BY SHAY HUNTER

Trembling, I shrugged and looked at the closed door. "I don't know. Guess I'll find out later."

She frowned and through squinted eyes said, "Why I don't believe you?"

"Why is it that everyone looks at me like I'm the bad guy? Why can't people see all I want to do is —"

KNOCK. KNOCK. KNOCK.

"I'll get it." Kaden walked to the door and I followed her and flopped on the living room sofa. On the other side of the door were my cousins Sahira and Georgia. They pushed their way inside and walked up to me with their usual attitudes.

Big and pretty they took up the living room with their large frames and larger personalities. Sahira was the wildest and the most deadly. She had cornrows running down her back and a mouth full of gold teeth. Georgia was the quieter of the two but just as bad with the large puff sitting on top of her head that she kept fluffing with her fingers every now and again.

"Aye, I just saw your nigga outside with Tabitha." Sahira said pointing at the door with her thumb. "You want me to break that up or nah?"

"Yeah, you letting that shit go down?" Georgia asked. "On your watch?"

I sighed. "We got other shit to worry about now." I stood up. "Follow me to my room." When the twins and Kaden were inside I closed and locked my bedroom door. "So I been going over a couple of ways to do this murder thing so we have to pick the best."

Georgia cracked her knuckles. "What you talking 'bout? I thought you said we were beating her to death."

"Nah, that's too messy," I said waving the air. "It's got to be cleaner."

"Can we at least beat her ass first and then do whatever?" Sahira suggested. "I'm just saying, I want to have a little fun especially after seeing her outside with Dandre." She stepped closer as if I couldn't hear her loud ass. "Do you know that nigga had the nerve to not even speak to me when I came into the building?"

"If it will make you feel better than have at it, Sahira," I said. "I don't even care as long as she's not breathing by the end of the night."

"I think that will be dumb." Kaden said in a low voice. "To fight her first."

Sahira frowned at her like she didn't even know she was in the room. "Why you say that? And what the fuck is wrong with your hair? Why it's not done?"

She looked at me. "Paris never got a chance to finish braiding it. She got locked up." She stared at Sahira. "Anyway, if you fight her you gonna get DNA under your nails," Kaden continued. "Now if you wanna go to jail it's whatever. Just leave me out of it."

Sahira looked at me while pointing at Kaden. "Why she in this plan again? Because she don't seem like a team player to me."

"Because we need all the help we can get," I said. "Now lets go over the ways to get this bitch." I walked to the left side of my bed and grabbed a piece of paper and unfolded it. "We could stab her. That would be quick."

"Again, too messy," Kaden said rolling her eyes. "Blood spurts everywhere."

I nodded and focused on the paper again. "Maybe you right. We can shoot her."

"Too loud," Kaden said rolling her eyes. "And the blood spurts again."

"Or we can poison her," I said.

We all looked at Kaden.

"What you gonna say about that?" Sahira said. "Since you got something negative to say about everything."

"They test for poison when somebody as young as her dies." She paused. "We gotta think of another plan."

"I got one," Sahira said as her eyes brightened. "Yah get that bitch in here and I'll choke her to death. Then we can make it look like she hung herself."

"You think that will work?" I asked, liking the idea.

"Somebody said her first husband hung himself. Maybe she still feels bad about that. At least that's what the people will think." Her eyes glistened and finally somebody on my team was getting me excited. "If you ask me with the right set up it'll work! Trust Sahira."

CHAPTER TWENTY-THREE

TABITHA

I was a little cool being outside and then Dandre handed me his jacket and stared down at me. What was wrong with him, besides telling me once again that he didn't want to marry Barby? At this point I could care less if he decided to be with her I just wanted him to leave me out of it or else he was gonna fuck up my shit.

"What she do this time, Dandre?" I asked with my arms folded in front of me. "Because for real this is getting old now." I looked up the block again to make sure I didn't see Chaviv coming.

"She did your friend wrong. I'm talking about Paris." He nodded. "It was her who called the police just so you know."

My eyebrows rose and I giggled.

"What's funny?" He frowned.

"Why you so concerned about that, Dandre? Even if she did do somebody wrong what business of it is yours? And what that got to do with yah relationship?"

"Because I can't marry no broad like that."

I giggled again. "Yeah, okay."

His neck corded. "What's funny now?"

"I think you making excuses. You didn't wanna give her the ring a while ago and you don't wanna give it to her now. If that's how you feel then just say it and be honest." I looked behind him and then myself before waiting for his answer.

He stood tall, chin up in the air but eyes still on me. "Okay...I wanna say and be honest 'bout something else that I don't think you can handle." He took a deep breath. "Or maybe you can if what Barby says is true. About you being jealous and all."

Fuck was he talking about. "I'm waiting."

He swallowed. "I'm feeling you too. Not a little but a lot."

My jaw dropped. "Ah, nah, not now, Dandre. You can't be doing this right now. You just can't."

He touched my shoulders before I knocked his hands off. "I know it's fucked up and I would never come at you like this but it's been how I felt from the gate."

"What about marrying Barby?"

"The whole proposal thing I created to get you alone. I figured if someone saw us together, I could

BY SHAY HUNTER

whip out the ring and show it was all about Barby. But ain't nobody trying to marry that scandalous bitch."

"Dandre, I don't feel that way about you." I paused. "And even if I did I'm in a relationship."

"Come on, man, you know Chaviv ain't 'bout you for real." He laughed and waved the air.

I frowned. "Why you say that?"

His hands clenched and unclenched. "Look at how he treats you. He says he's gonna be somewhere and then when you wait for him he don't show up. He says he's gonna bring something for you and it falls through." He touched my shoulders. "If I was in his shoes I would never do that to you. Come on, Tabitha, give a nigga a chance. I ain't the prettiest but I can be the best to you. And you deserve a nice nigga."

I laughed. "Dandre, you don't know nothing 'bout me. Nice and my name shouldn't go in the same sentence."

"Well that's even better because I like a hood bitch. And I still know what kind of woman you are." He moved closer as if he wasn't close enough. "We adults, Tabitha. Whatever we do can stay between us."

"The fact that you can even think about me that way means I've given you the wrong impression and that's fucked up. But I'm not interested."

He nodded. "So you playing me like a clown?"

"What?" My eyes widened. "You stepped to me not—"

"You been tossing your pussy 'round me for months. And now when I come to you, you gonna fake like you don't want a nigga?" He paused. "Like you can't give a nigga a little bit of pussy so he won't feel stupid 'bout himself?"

"Dandre, you need to stay as far away from me as possible. Trust me when I say I'm doing you a favor."

CHAVIV

When Chaviv pulled up and saw Dandre with Tabitha outside he had enough heat on him to blast them both into space. His temples throbbed and he felt played as he watched Dandre place his hands on her as if he belonged to her and not him.

And then there was Tabitha.

206   BY SHAY HUNTER

Who did she think she was to fuck another nigga under his nose? With the entire neighborhood knowing? Didn't she realize what kind of man he was?

The females she lived with told him that Tabitha was fucking old boy but he wasn't trying to believe the truth. Now he could see it clear as the gun in his lap.

In his opinion Dandre couldn't blame it on the wedding ring because he already copped it. It wasn't like he was asking her to help him plan the ceremony.

He turned his music up and pulled in front of the building to separate the duo. Both of them faced Chaviv's ride and looked guilty as he parked. Taking a deep breath, Chaviv eased out of his truck and bopped up to Tabitha, his hands in his pockets.

Once upon them, Dandre tried to shake his hand but Chaviv wasn't having any of it. He was done being polite.

"What you doing out here, bae?" He asked looking at her with his back faced him. "I thought you'd be getting ready for your party upstairs."

"I...I did, I mean I am." She looked at Dandre who hadn't bothered to walk away although she wanted him to. "Was just talking to Dandre about when he was proposing."

Chaviv smiled at her although he still hadn't bothered to acknowledge Dandre. "You mean you still gotta help this *nigga out? Seems to me the real work is done. Either he gonna marry the bitch or not." Now he looked at Dandre. "Why you need so much time with my girl on the matter? Seems off to me."*

Dandre cleared his throat. "I'm goin' upstairs to see if they need anything for the party."

"You do that," Chaviv said.

"We right behind you," Tabitha said to Dandre.

The moment he left Chaviv tore into her like a madman. "What I tell you 'bout keeping time with this nigga? Huh?" He frowned. "What I tell you 'bout talking to this nigga on the solo?"

"Chaviv – "

"Answer the question!"

She shook her head. "I think you got the wrong impression about me. I care about you, Chaviv and I couldn't fuck around on you like that. You know that right?"

"Yeah, aight. Whatever happens to that nigga is on you." He pointed at her and walked away.

TABITHA

BY SHAY HUNTER

A few hours later the party was in full motion.

Things were tense in the house and it was perfect for my plans to unfold. Chaviv made what felt like a threat and Dandre was getting on my nerves staring at me across the room.

When one of my neighbors walked up to me I knew it was time to kick things to the next level. "Girl, this party is nice," Carol from upstairs said. I could smell her dirty hair weave and tried to hide my disgust. "I think it's so cute that you did this for your roommates."

Suddenly I broke out into tears and she hugged me. Great, now I smelled her underarms too. Didn't she know how to wash? "What's wrong, Tabitha? Everything is so nice. The chicken is a little salty but it's aight."

I separated from her and wiped my tears. "Girl, I'm so scared. Everybody around here is fighting. Chaviv threatened my roommates lives and I don't know what to do. I think one of them may get killed."

She rubbed my back but I could feel she was trying to get away from me to tell everyone in the party what she knew.

Mission halfway accomplished.

BY SHAY HUNTER

CHAPTER TWENTY-FOUR
BARBY

I sat in the room with my cousins and Kaden waiting for the situation to fall in place. I was loading my gun just in case, even though the idea was a good firm choking. Sahira was stuffing the pillow with extra clothes which we were gonna use as a silencer if nobody could squeeze the life out of Tabitha.

I was getting excited about the money that would come my way when I saw Kaden looking crazy in the corner of my room. Like she lost her best friend and couldn't find her. I knew what her problem really was, somebody told her that Dandre was proposing to me which was why Tabitha had been spending so much time with him. And now she felt guilty.

"Look, I don't care if she was only helping Dandre propose to me, Kaden. She still acting dirty."

Her eyes widened and slowly her head rotated in my direction. "Hold up...what you talking about?" She walked toward me. "What you mean Dandre was proposing to you?"

I rolled my eyes and breathed in her face because I hated repeating myself. "I said I don't care if she was talking to him about the ring. Which supposedly explained why they spent so much time together." I sighed. "At this point I want this money."

She covered her mouth and I realized at that moment she didn't know. Fuck! I shouldn't have said anything. When she looked like she was about to run out of the room I stuffed the gun under the pillow and grabbed her. People were already in the living room for the party and she was 'bout to blow up my set.

I closed the door again.

"So Tabitha didn't tell you? About the proposal? I thought that was the reason you were looking crazy in the mirror."

"You started all of this drama over Dandre and all Tabitha was doing was helping him propose to you? Don't you feel wrong about any of this?" Tears rolled down her cheek. "How could you be so cold?"

I shrugged. "I'm sure she did something else, Kaden. The girl is evil! I know it when I see it. Maybe it's because I am too. I can't be sure. But she deserves to die. Now let's not play the Real Housewives of Atlanta."

She tried to walk past me and Sahira stopped her this time. "Where you going long legs? It's almost time for action and we need all team players on deck."

"I'm not gonna be a part of this," Kaden said looking at all of us. "I'm not gonna hurt somebody innocent."

"But I thought you said Lakota wanted to move in with you," I reminded her as I watched Sahira stand behind her and braid Kaden's last piece of hair without asking. It was creepy too because Kaden winced and I loved it. "How you gonna do that when he ain't got no money and scared to pump on the streets?"

She squinted a little because Sahira was braiding that shit tight, I could tell. "We gonna make it work," Kaden whispered.

"Really?" I stepped in front of her. "And how you gonna do that?"

"Barby, you have started so much shit since you been here," Kaden said. "You pointed out a few things that Tabitha did but what about you and your shit?"

I put my hands on my hips. "What you talking about?"

"Where is your rent money? I checked the banking account and you didn't deposit it like we did."

I blinked a few times. "It doesn't matter. We moving in a place of our own remember?"

"But where is your part on the bill?"

Sahira had finished braiding her hair and looked at me.

I shrugged. "The question is dumb, Kaden. The last thing I'm thinking 'bout is rent money when I know we leaving."

"You know what, I realized something with you." She pointed at me. "Every time you don't have your rent money you start a fight with us or Dandre and threaten to leave. Usually I pay your way because I never wanted to find another roommate. But now...but now I finally get what's going on."

"Oh really. And what's that?"

She stepped so close our titties were touching. "That you the one we shouldn't trust. Not Tabitha."

"Bitch, you better step out my cousin's face." Sahira said stepping in front of her. "Before I snap your neck."

"Hold up, sis. I think Kaden is right," Georgia said fluffing her bush with her fingertips. "You do be starting fights when the rent due, Barby. Did it when you lived with me and Sahira too."

I looked at her. "So now you taking her side? Over your own flesh and blood?"

"It's not 'bout that," Georgia said. "It's about you being a trouble maker. Auntie said the same thing when I told her we were on our way up here. Told us to stay the fuck home and let you tend to your own business." She shook her head. "You did ask me to borrow some money a few days ago for rent. When I told you I didn't have it, the next thing I know we killing this bitch. It's like we went from zero to a hundred."

Kaden nodded. "Exactly, because she's greedy and selfish."

Sahira stepped up to Kaden and punched her in the stomach before pointing at her sister. "You not gonna fuck this up for me. I never had this amount of money and this my chance to be fly and rich for a change, Georgia. Don't make me hurt both of you." She looked at Kaden.

"I'm going to get some air," Kaden said holding her stomach.

I blocked her. "No you not. You ain't in no condition to do anything but lie down somewhere."

She rolled her eyes. "Listen, I was a little out of it mentally but now I'm back. All I need is some fresh air. I'm not going to the police or Tabitha."

"If you gonna get some air Sahira going with you."

Her eyebrows rose. "Wait...you serious?"

"Do it look like I'm playing?"

"Barby, I don't have time for this. I said I'm not going anywhere so stop—"

"Bitch, this is going down today. If you want me to trust you then you better be worthy of it first." She looked over my head at Sahira. "Now...let her go with you. She needs some air too."

Kaden rolled her eyes as she walked out the door with my cousin behind her like the warden in a prison. With the door closed me and Georgia placed everything we needed under the bed. When we were done Georgia asked, "So why you didn't volunteer me to go?"

"To go where, Georgia?" I stood up and checked my locs in the mirror.

"With Kaden outside to get some air?"

I laughed. "You don't have to ask me questions you already know the answer to with your, weak ass."

When there was a knock at my door I opened it. It was Dandre. "Listen, I want to tell you something." He looked behind me at Georgia. "In private."

"Let's go to Kaden's room," I smiled.

"What?" he looked over my shoulder and back at me. "Why can't we stay here?"

"Because Georgia taking care of something for me." I paused and grabbed his hand. "Come with me. Nobody in her room."

He followed me and we walked into Kaden's room, closing the door behind us. "What's up?" I was bracing myself for foolishness.

"I can't marry you." He looked away from me.

My jaw opened and closed several times. "What...why? Because of Paris? If that's the reason you wrong, Dandre. I can make a good wife. A nice wife."

"Nah. That ain't it."

"Then what is it?"

"Because I'm not feeling you."

I walked around the room before finally sitting on the edge of the bed. "Dandre, you can't do me like this. It's not fair." I cried. "You can't tell a person you marrying them and then change your mind like this. It's wrong, Dandre."

He frowned. "How the fuck you sound? I didn't tell you I was going to marry you. You found out and fucked your own head up."

"Were you really gonna marry me?"

"What?" He glared. "Fuck you talking about? You sound dumb."

"Because it doesn't make any sense how a person could want to be with someone forever and then change their mind so easily. I'm not understanding. Unless you really wanted Tabitha all along."

"There's nothing more I can say to you, Barby. You not the person I thought you was."

"So all the times you were running around with Tabitha, what was that about? You wanted her instead right? Just be honest for a fucking change!"

"Look, I'm staying for the party but beyond that I don't know what else to say." He shrugged. "Me and you gonna have to work on some things if we gonna make it. I'm out."

He walked out and when he opened the door Tabitha was looking at me, with a sly smile on her face.

Her look gave me chills.

All of this time I thought she was naive but now that look told me that she was something else.

Something worse than me.

Who are you really Tabitha?

CHAPTER TWENTY-FIVE

KADEN

I don't feel like celebrating...

There were so many people in our apartment now I could barely move around in the living room. I can't believe all of these people are here, none of them knowing that in a little while someone would be murdered.

I was on my third drink when Lakota bopped up to me like he was real cool. I can't believe he came. "Where Dandre?" When I looked behind him I saw his friend Perry was staring into my mouth. "He coming tonight right?"

I shrugged. "I'm not sure what he doing, Lakota." I looked down at his feet and saw new sneakers. What the fuck? I thought he was broke. "I like your shoes." I crossed my arms over my chest.

"You just got 'em?"

He smiled. "Yeah, I went to the..." He stopped talking, guess He remembered he was supposed to be broke and begging me for cash. "Fuck all that, you think Dandre coming or not?"

I rolled my eyes and crossed my arms tighter across my chest. My stomach still hurt from being punched and now my head was throbbing too. "I don't know...ask Barby."

He frowned and talked through clenched teeth. "I'm asking you."

I looked at him and his friend again who was still staring at my tonsils. They definitely were here for trouble. Why couldn't they do whatever on the streets? Why bring it in our apartment? "I really don't know, Lakota. That's all I can tell you."

He nodded. "But he definitely 'spose to be coming tonight right?"

Was he even listening? I said the same thing over and over. Suddenly he grossed me out. When I looked at him up and down I realized he was everything I thought I wanted which obviously meant I had no taste. Instead of answering I got up and walked away from him.

He grabbed my arm just as I entered my room. "Wait...why you bounce off like that?" he looked back at his friend. "You trying to embarrass me or something? What I tell you about that type shit?"

I snatched away from him. "Get out of my face. And get the fuck out of my life."

"What? Who you—"

"Lakota, I asked you once I'm not gonna ask again. Now there are a lot of bitches in here. Find one of them, any one, and bother them instead. I'm done with your dry ass." I slammed the door in his face.

LAKOTA

Lakota walked back into the party after talking to Kaden. He shook his head at the disrespect Kaden threw his way because she never argued at him like that.

But like always he pretended he didn't care.

Still, it was peculiar how she could go from wanting to be with him to wanting to be left alone in the same day. He just never saw a woman who was finally fed up but he had in that moment.

"I thought you said that was your girl," Perry, his friend, said the moment Lakota stood next to him looking stupid. Perry was dancing with one of their next-door

neighbors who was carrying on as if she were trying to get a baby out the dance.

"Fuck that bitch," Lakota said grabbing the beer he left on the table. "She want somebody to chase her ass and I'm not 'bout to do it." Perry nodded and grabbed the girl's ass in front of him. "She'll be on my dick later though.

"I thought you said she look like a nigga."

"She do sometimes."

Perry laughed. "I guess you don't got no taste. If I saw her I would've pulled up on her."

Now Lakota felt extra dumb.

"Anyway, what she say about Dandre?" Perry continued. "She give any details? Cuz I'm burning this nigga skull the moment I lay eyes on 'em."

"Nah, she ain't say nothing...just that he wasn't here." Lakota looked at the door again. "Stupid, bitch."

"So you wanna stay around waiting for him?" He cuffed the bitch's loose stank ass again. "Or you trying to go to that other party out Southwest?"

Lakota looked at him and smiled. "What you think, nigga? I think he been dodging me but now he ain't got no choice but to pop up here. Everybody know he trying to fuck Tabitha's fine ass. I'm waiting."

Perry nodded. "Aye, man, I'm with you, all you gotta do is say the word. The rest will fall in place."

TABITHA

I just finished doing the last thing I was going to do ever for this party. Everybody had food, drinks and even weed edibles, courtesy of the work I put in all week long.

Now it was time for me to grab a drink, sit back and wait for shit to go my way. I expected to see Chaviv even though he faked like he had an attitude earlier when he walked me into the apartment. There was no way he was gonna let a bunch of niggas hang around me, especially Dandre. I hadn't seen Dandre and the only one of our boyfriends here was Lakota. And I figured Kaden was in her room about to be up under him in any minute.

I was watching the neighbors dance and talk about how good the food was when Barby stepped up to me. "Can I talk to you for a minute, Tabitha?" She was loud enough to be heard over the music but not loud enough for everyone else to hear. "In private?"

I frowned. "What's wrong?"

"Why something gotta be wrong for me to talk to you?" She played with one of her locs.

I shrugged. "Barby, we ain't been having no real words for each other all week. And now you want to keep time with me." I shook my head. "Seems odd is all."

"Just because we don't talk don't mean we ain't friends do it? Besides, I been trying to kick it with you for the past week but all you wanted to do was play Martha Stewart in the kitchen, so I left you to it." She paused. "Now stop messing around and come talk to me in my room. It can't wait."

"Aight." I stood up to follow her to her room when all of a sudden the music stopped. I turned around to see what happened and saw Carol from upstairs looking guilty. Everybody was mad when the music stopped and let it be known in their sounds.

"I'm sorry, Tabitha!" She said holding my iPad. "I was trying to put another song on. People tired of Trap music."

"Bitch, take your dumb ass upstairs!" Somebody yelled. "The music was right up in this bitch!"

I shook my head. "Give me a second, Barby," I told her. "I gotta connect the music back up to the Bluetooth speakers.

"Aight, I'll be in my room. Come right in when you finish."

She walked away and I stomped over to my neighbor. "Girl, you don't mess with nobody's music." I pause. "You ask first!"

"I was trying to slow it down a little." She looked across the room. "Plus I'm feeling dude over there. Figured he'd want to take me home if the right song came on."

I looked in the direction she was staring in. The party was pretty packed but for the most part the person standing out was Lakota. "You not talking about that dude with the blue jeans and white t-shirt are you?"

"Yeah, he fine as shit ain't he?" She licked her lips.

I laughed. "Unless you trying to fight tonight leave him alone, Carol." I paused. "He go with my roommate."

She frowned. "I doubt that."

"Listen, I see the nigga almost every other day in this apartment. Trust me when I say they together."

"Maybe it's how it used to be but when I pushed up on him he said he was single. Now I don't know your roommate all that well but he sounded like he was available to me."

I turned the music back to my trap playlist. I wasn't about to slow nothing down for her or rap to her anymore. Not only that, I wanted to talk to Lakota. But right before I walked up to him I saw Kaden go into Barby's room.

Barby looked over at me and said, "Come on, girl. We waiting on you."

I threw one finger up. "Give me a second."

I figured they were trying to have a roommate meeting, which I wasn't feeling one bit. I had other things on my mind. When she closed the door I walked up to Lakota. "So you cheating on Kaden now in her apartment?"

He smirked. "Why you say that?"

"Because she—"

When I turned around I saw Dandre, Keith and Mo-Mo walking into the house. Behind him was Chaviv who had a gaze on his face I didn't like.

"Tabitha, can you come in here for a second!" Barby yelled at me standing in her room's doorway again. "It's serious and can't wait."

I had so much going on that I decided to go talk to her to get it over with. The moment I stepped to the door and glanced inside I saw her cousins and Kaden looking crazy in my direction. I was halfway in her room when Chaviv walked up to me, grabbed my arm, yanked me back and looked into my eyes.

"Are you serious about me?" He asked. He smelled of alcohol and some other drug I wasn't familiar with. Now that I think about it, he may have been doing dippers, which meant he was way beyond crazy in that moment. "I need to know right now."

"What? Of course I'm serious about you and our relationship. Why you say that?" I asked.

"Come talk to me when you finish with him," Barby said with an attitude. "It's important."

I turned toward her. "What? Oh...yeah. I'll be right in." I forgot she was even standing there.

She closed the door.

"Then why I feel like you playing me for that nigga, Tabitha?" Chaviv continued. "Huh?"

I shrugged. "Maybe you the one holding something back." I admitted. "I'm not—"

"Tabitha, I think the landlord wants you to come downstairs," my neighbor who was just trying to change the music yelled at me from the front door. "She said you gotta come down now."

"Give me a second, Chaviv," I said to him. "I'll be right back when I find out what my landlord wants because I already told her about this party."

I turned to leave and when I was in the hallway I locked the door, ran down the steps and pushed the door open to the building.

My sister Lexi was standing there with a smile on her face. "Bitch, what took you so long?" I asked walking quickly to her car. "All kinds of shit about to take off in there."

"I had to drop your nigga off first after fucking up his mind," Lexi winked. "I think you were smart about letting him do the work instead of me."

"Yeah, cause all we need is one dead to get the check, we'll get the others later." I paused. "So what you say to Chaviv? He mad as fuck."

"All kinds of shit. That you fucking behind his back and that niggas, especially Barby, is playing him stupid. Girl, I repeated that shit over and over and then gave him a Dipper. He gonna hurt something tonight, trust me. And you don't need to be nowhere near him."

I smiled. "I think this one is gonna pay out, Lexi." I said with squinted eyes.

We both hopped into the car. "Well that's your stupid ass roommates for you. We been doing this long enough to know that can't nobody push drama on you but yourself. If anything they could've walked away at anytime and they didn't. Now they gotta pay for it not knowing that you set all this shit up."

We both laughed and pulled off.

CHAPTER TWENTY-SIX
THE PARTY

*N*o one in the party knew Tabitha was gone...
How could they?

She had filled them with weed, food, and more than anything lies. And now Tabitha was waiting for her big pay day.

Ready to settle old beef, Dandre stepped up to Lakota and said, "So I heard you been looking for me."

Lakota laughed and observed Mo-Mo and Keith behind him who he was already aware of that caused drama in the streets. "Is that what you heard? Because I heard the same thing."

"Stop fucking around nigga," Dandre said louder. "It's not a game for me. You stabbed me in the hand and then send your girl to beg you back into my graces."

Lakota laughed. "Is that what she said? If she did she got it wrong."

Dandre shrugged.

"All I want to know is why you killed my cousin?" Lakota asked. "You been telling everybody but me and we were close at one point."

Dandre laughed. "The niggas robbed my man right here," he said pointing at Mo-Mo. "And we got tired of him bragging about it in DC. Just like I'm tired of talking now."

Dandre hit Lakota in the mouth, and shattered his teeth. Blood spewed everywhere and that one blow lead to a full fledge fight in the living room. The second for the week.

BARBY

I was watching Kaden chant over and over why we shouldn't kill Tabitha because she didn't do anything. She was getting on my nerves. "Tonight is gonna be bad," she shook her head. "Tonight gonna be real bad." She paused. "Maybe we should leave her alone. Something tells me to leave her alone and leave this apartment."

"Listen, I'm not leaving her alone and you not leaving this apartment!" I yelled. "So stop asking. Put your mind at ease by realizing that ain't happening."

"At this point it's dumb to try and back out anyway," Sahira shrugged. "We already got the groundwork laid. Now we just waiting on our prey." She looked at the door and rubbed her hands together.

"So why isn't she here yet?" Kaden asked. "Anybody thought about that? Maybe she's on to us. Maybe she got cameras in here or something and knows it's coming."

When I heard yelling outside I put my hand up and said, "Hold up?" I was trying to listen because I thought I heard yelling over the music. "What's all that screaming?" I pulled my door open and I saw Dandre and Lakota on the floor fighting with everyone standing around watching and cheering. Most of our neighbors left and the only people there were Dandre, Lakota, Chaviv and their friends.

I rushed up to them and I could feel Sahira and Georgia walking behind me. "What's going on?" I asked trying to break them up. "Why yah Fighting this time? Please stop this shit!"

No one answered. Instead I saw Dandre remove a gun from his jeans and fire into Lakota's chest. Blood splashed on my mouth as I watched him drop.

It felt like the room was spinning. For a second the only thing I could hear was Kaden's loud cries as she dropped to her knees and tried to lift Lakota's limp body.

I felt like I was in a scary movie as Chaviv walked to the door, locked it and held a gun to the back of Dandre's head before squeezing the trigger. Lakota's friend Perry tried to leave and Chaviv shot him before killing Mo-Mo and Keith when they tried to escape also.

At that time I noticed Chaviv's eyes were rolling all around his head as he was reloading his gun. He looked insane like he was on something.

Now it was just me, Kaden and my cousins. He wiped the sweat away that fell into his eyes. "Yah two bitches started a lot of shit, you know that?" He said to me and Kaden.

I put my hands up and could hear my cousins whimper. "I don't know what you talking about, Chaviv. We real cool with you."

"You know what I'm talking about. And there ain't no way I'm letting you get out of here alive." First he shot Kaden who was still on the floor, distraught over Lakota's death and then he shot my cousins Georgia and Sahira who tried to run into my room.

I peed on myself and it ran down my inner thighs and onto the floor.

"I realize something about you." He pointed the gun at me. "You caused more problems then anybody I ever met. You know that?"

"I'm sorry...I just..."

"Just what? Like to keep shit up?" he paused. "I warned you bitch and now —"

Without another word he shot me.

From the distance I could hear the police coming and was slightly relieved that I would survive until things went dark and I could no longer breathe.

EPILOGUE

FOUR MONTHS LATER

Tabitha and her sister Lexi looked around their new apartment in Miami Florida. When Tabitha opened her living room curtain she smiled at how the ocean sparkled before her eyes.

After the murders, which were blamed on Chaviv, a crazed mad man with a warrant for his arrest, a check in the amount of $100,000 for a business Tabitha and her roommates no longer owned was written in Tabitha's name.

Chaviv was eventually charged for the homicides of nine people and arrested and he vowed revenge on Tabitha when he learned of the payout.

Since that was their third time running the insurance scheme, with a different insurance company of course, they knew they were officially out of the insurance scam business. Now they had to set their sights on some bigger money that had no paper trail.

Drug dealers.

As they reflected on the recent payout they realized their plan, like the others, was simple.

First, have Lexi look through criminal records at her job as a Parole Officer in Washington DC, for the perfect mentally unstable thug.

Second, arrange to meet with said crazy man and seduce him at a Go-Go, which Tabitha did the day she wore jeans so tight she had to scrape them off and Chaviv could not resist.

Third, rent a big beautiful apartment and get roommates with bad credit history, who couldn't get a place that nice on their own. That part was unfortunately easy.

Fourth, appear harmless by having the crazy man, aka Chaviv, come over on a regular basis to see her and to stay in the kitchen cooking. That way the roommates could see Tabitha wasn't interested in their men and would trust her believing she was harmless.

Fifth, suggest a business that would fail and have a lawyer suggest life insurance, which was procedural for people creating a business together. When the business failed, what Tabitha needed to do was add the fee to her rent so that the roommates would not care or even think about it being open. Besides, the harmless person she made herself out to be meant that Tabitha could fly under the radar for the vested period of eight months the policy called for.

Sixth, strike up confusion with the roommates concerning their men. This was just incase the seventh part of her plan didn't work, and she could use one of the roommates as a scapegoat for the murders.

Seventh, have the sister fuck crazy man, get the gun with his prints and fill his head with lies, before taking the gun for the murders later.

Now here is where the plan changed in Tabitha and Lexi's favor. The eighth part of the plan called for Lexi to kill each of the roommates using Chaviv's gun that would have his prints. But when they detected a major emotional weakness in him they shifted the plan a little. They would have him actually commit the murder of at least Barby since he hated her so much. And right before the payout, which would include Kaden and Paris getting paid also, Lexi would kill them and Tabitha's payout would be bigger. The fact that Lakota and Dandre had beef over street shit was a bonus.

The only flaw was Paris who was in prison on manslaughter charges for ten years. Her portion had to go to Maceo's family since they sued. Which was why when Tabitha learned she was locked up, did her best to get her out to kill her too.

While eating steak on the deck Lexi asked Tabitha, "Do you feel bad for what we did to them?"

Tabitha smiled. "You mean my roommates?" She giggled.

"Yeah."

"What did we do?" Tabitha giggled. "Unlike the others we didn't pull the trigger. All I did was flirt a little with their men to get them beefing which they allowed me to do. A stronger woman would've left the apartment two months before the murders happened, after I flashed my asses to their men." She giggled. "But they were too blinded by the fancy crib and the food to leave." She shrugged. "And the murder, well, we all know who was responsible for that."

Lexi sipped her drink. "Poor, Chaviv." With a piece of steak in her mouth she asked, "So what do we do now?"

"I'm thinking of something more fun…" She looked out at the city. "Miami is famous for it's dope, let's find ourselves a rich dope boy and take him for all they got."

"It won't be as easy as the others." Lexi warned. "You know that right?"

"Who cares, we ready," she winked.

"I love you, big sis."

"I love you, too." Tabitha raised a glass in the air. "Almost as much as I do this money."

They giggled and plotted their next adventure.

CARTEL PUBLICATIONS
PRESENTS

The Cartel Publications Order Form

www.thecartelpublications.com

Inmates **ONLY** receive novels for $10.00 per book.
(Mail Order **MUST** come from inmate directly to receive discount)

Shyt List 1	_____	$15.00
Shyt List 2	_____	$15.00
Shyt List 3	_____	$15.00
Shyt List 4	_____	$15.00
Shyt List 5	_____	$15.00
Pitbulls In A Skirt	_____	$15.00
Pitbulls In A Skirt 2	_____	$15.00
Pitbulls In A Skirt 3	_____	$15.00
Pitbulls In A Skirt 4	_____	$15.00
Pitbulls In A Skirt 5	_____	$15.00
Victoria's Secret	_____	$15.00
Poison 1	_____	$15.00
Poison 2	_____	$15.00
Hell Razor Honeys	_____	$15.00
Hell Razor Honeys 2	_____	$15.00
A Hustler's Son	_____	$15.00
A Hustler's Son 2	_____	$15.00
Black and Ugly	_____	$15.00
Black and Ugly As Ever	_____	$15.00
Year Of The Crackmom	_____	$15.00
Deadheads	_____	$15.00
The Face That Launched A	_____	$15.00
Thousand Bullets		
The Unusual Suspects	_____	$15.00
Miss Wayne & The Queens of DC	_____	$15.00
Paid In Blood (eBook Only)	_____	$15.00
Raunchy	_____	$15.00
Raunchy 2	_____	$15.00
Raunchy 3	_____	$15.00
Mad Maxxx	_____	$15.00
Quita's Dayscare Center	_____	$15.00
Quita's Dayscare Center 2	_____	$15.00
Pretty Kings	_____	$15.00
Pretty Kings 2	_____	$15.00
Pretty Kings 3	_____	$15.00
Pretty Kings 4	_____	$15.00
Silence Of The Nine	_____	$15.00
Silence Of The Nine 2	_____	$15.00
Prison Throne	_____	$15.00
Drunk & Hot Girls	_____	$15.00
Hersband Material	_____	$15.00
The End: How To Write A	_____	$15.00
Bestselling Novel In 30 Days (Non-Fiction Guide)		
Upscale Kittens	_____	$15.00
Wake & Bake Boys	_____	$15.00
Young & Dumb	_____	$15.00
Young & Dumb 2:	_____	$15.00
Tranny 911	_____	$15.00

Tranny 911: Dixie's Rise	_____	$15.00
First Comes Love, Then Comes Murder	_____	$15.00
Luxury Tax	_____	$15.00
The Lying King	_____	$15.00
Crazy Kind Of Love	_____	$15.00
And They Call Me God	_____	$15.00
The Ungrateful Bastards	_____	$15.00
Lipstick Dom	_____	$15.00
A School of Dolls	_____	$15.00
Hoetic Justice	_____	$15.00
KALI: Raunchy Relived	_____	$15.00
Skeezers	_____	$15.00
You Kissed Me, Now I Own You	_____	$15.00
Nefarious	_____	$15.00
Redbone 3: The Rise of The Fold	_____	$15.00
Clown Niggas	_____	$15.00
The One You Shouldn't Trust	_____	$15.00

(**Redbone 1 & 2** are **NOT** Cartel Publications novels and if **ordered** the cost is **FULL** price of $15.00 **each. No Exceptions**.)

Please add $5.00 **PER BOOK** for shipping and handling.

The Cartel Publications * P.O. BOX 486 OWINGS MILLS MD 21117

Name: _____

Address: _____

City/State: _____

Contact/Email: _____

Please allow 5-7 BUSINESS days before shipping.

The Cartel Publications is NOT responsible for Prison Orders rejected, NO RETURNS and NO REFUNDS.

NO PERSONAL CHECKS ACCEPTED

STAMPS NO LONGER ACCEPTED

BY SHAY HUNTER

CPSIA information can be obtained
at www.ICGtesting.com
Printed in the USA
LVOW08s1502140417
530891LV00001B/110/P